GOING SOME
A ROMANCE OF STRENUOUS AFFECTION

By
REX BEACH

Going Some
A Romance Of Strenuous Affection

by Rex Beach

Copyright © 2023

All Rights reserved.
No part of this publication may be reproduced, stored in a retrieval system, or transmitted in any form or by any means, electronic, mechanical, photocopying or Otherwise, without the written permission of the publisher.

The author/editor asserts the moral right to be identified as the author/editor of this work.

ISBN: 978-93-57273-44-2

Published by

DOUBLE 9 BOOKS

2/13-B, Ansari Road, Daryaganj
New Delhi – 110002
info@double9books.com
www.double9books.com
Tel. 011-40042856

This book is under public domain

ABOUT THE AUTHOR

Rex Ellingwood Beach (September 1, 1877 - December 7, 1949) was an American novelist, playwright, and Olympic water polo player. He was born in Atwood, Michigan, but moved to Tampa, Florida, with his family where his father was growing fruit trees. Beach was educated at Rollins College, Florida (1891-1896), the Chicago College of Law (1896-97), and Kent College of Law, Chicago (1899-1900). In 1900 he was drawn to Alaska at the time of the Klondike Gold Rush. After five years of unsuccessful prospecting, he turned to writing. His second novel The Spoilers (1906) was based on a true story of corrupt government officials stealing gold mines from prospectors, which he witnessed while he was prospecting in Nome, Alaska. The Spoilers became one of the bestselling novels of 1906.

CONTENTS

CHAPTER I 7

CHAPTER II 14

CHAPTER III 22

CHAPTER IV 30

CHAPTER V 38

CHAPTER VI 45

CHAPTER VII 55

CHAPTER VIII 63

CHAPTER IX 71

CHAPTER X 80

CHAPTER XI 88

CHAPTER XII 95

CHAPTER XIII 105

CHAPTER XIV 112

CHAPTER XV 122

CHAPTER XVI 134

CHAPTER XVII 142

CHAPTER XVIII 152

CHAPTER I

Four cowboys inclined their bodies over the barbed-wire fence which marked the dividing-line between the Centipede Ranch and their own, staring mournfully into a summer night such as only the far southwestern country knows. Big yellow stars hung thick and low — so low that it seemed they might almost be plucked by an upstretched hand — and a silent air blew across thousands of open miles of land lying crisp and fragrant under the velvet dark.

And as the four inclined their bodies, they inclined also their ears, after the strained manner of listeners who feel anguish at what they hear. A voice, shrill and human, pierced the night like a needle, then, with a wail of a tortured soul, died away amid discordant raspings: the voice of a phonograph. It was their own, or had been until one overconfident day, when the Flying Heart Ranch had risked it as a wager in a foot-race with the neighboring Centipede, and their own man had been too slow. As it had been their pride, it remained their disgrace. Dearly had they loved, and dearly lost it. It meant something that looked like honor, and though there were ten thousand thousand phonographs, in all the world there was not one that could take its place.

The sound ceased, there was an approving distant murmur of men's voices, and then the song began:

"Jerusalem, Jerusalem,
Lift up your voice and sing—"

Higher and higher the voice mounted until it reached again its first thin, ear-splitting pitch.

"Still Bill" Stover stirred uneasily in the darkness. "Why 'n 'ell don't they keep her wound up?" he complained. "Gallagher's got the soul of a wart-hog. It's criminal the way he massacres that hymn."

From a rod farther down the wire fence Willie answered him, in a boy's falsetto:

"I wonder if he does it to spite me?"

"He don't know you're here," said Stover.

The other came out of the gloom, a little stoop-shouldered man with spectacles.

"I ain't noways sure," he piped, peering up at his lanky foreman. "Why do you reckon he allus lets Mrs. Melby peter out on my favorite record? He done the same thing last night. It looks like an insult."

"It's nothing but ignorance," Stover replied. "He don't want no trouble with you. None of 'em do."

"I'd like to know for certain." The small man seemed torn by doubt. "If I only knew he done it a-purpose, I'd git him. I bet I could do it from here."

Stover's voice was gruff as he commanded: "Forget it! Ain't it bad enough for us fellers to hang around like this every night without advertising our idiocy by a gun-play?"

"They ain't got no right to that phonograph," Willie averred, darkly.

"Oh yes, they have; they won it fair and square."

"Fair and square! Do you mean to say Humpy Joe run that foot-race on the square?"

"I never said nothin' like that whatever. I mean we bet it, and we lost it. Listen! There goes Carara's piece!"

Out past the corral floated the announcement in a man's metallic syllables:

"The Baggage Coach Ahead, as sung by Helena Mora for the Echo Phonograph, of New York and Pa-a-aris!"

From the dusk to the right of the two listeners now issued soft Spanish phrases.

"Madre de Dios! 'The Baggage Car in Front!' T'adora Mora! God bless 'er!"

During the rendition of this affecting ballad the two cow-men remained draped uncomfortably over the barbed-wire barrier, lost in rapturous enjoyment. When the last note had died away, Stover roused himself reluctantly.

"It's time we was turnin' in." He called softly, "Hey, Mex!"

"Si, Senor!"

"Come on, you and Cloudy. Vamos! It's ten o'clock."

He turned his back on the Centipede Ranch that housed the treasure, and in company with Willie, made his way to the ponies. Two other figures joined them, one humming in a musical baritone the strains of the song just ended.

"Cut that out, Mex! They'll hear us," Stover cautioned.

"Caramba! This t'ing is brek my 'eart," said the Mexican, sadly. "It seem like the Senorita Mora is sing that song to me. Mebbe she knows I'm set out 'ere on cactus an' listen to her. Ah, I love that Senorita ver' much."

The little man with the glasses began to swear in his high falsetto. His ear had caught the phonograph operator in another musical mistake.

"That horn-toad let Mrs. Melby die again to-night," said he. "It's sure comin' to a runnacaboo between him and me. If somebody don't kill him pretty soon, he'll wear out that machine before we git it back."

"Humph! It don't look like we'd ever get it back," said Stover.

One of the four sighed audibly, then vaulting into his saddle, went loping away without waiting for his companions.

"Cloudy's sore because they didn't play Navajo," said Willie. "Well, I don't blame 'em none for omittin' that war-dance. It ain't got the class of them other pieces. While it's devised to suit the intellect of an Injun, perhaps; it ain't in the runnin' with The Holy City, which tune is the sweetest and sacredest ever sung."

Carara paused with a hand upon the neck of his cayuse.

"Ect is not so fine as The Baggage Car in Front," he declared.

"It's got it beat a mile!" Willie flashed back, harshly.

"Here you!" exclaimed Stover, "no arguments. We all have our favorites, and it ain't up to no individual to force his likes and dislikes down no other feller's throat." The two men he addressed mounted their broncos stiffly.

"I repeat," said Willie: "The Holy City, as sung by Mrs. Melby, is the swellest tune that ever hit these parts."

Carara muttered something in Spanish which the others could not understand.

"They're all fine pieces," Stover observed, placatingly, when fairly out of hearing of the ranch-houses. "You boys have each got your preference. Cloudy, bein' an Injun, has got his, and I rise to state that I like that monologue, Silas on Fifth Avenoo, better than all of 'em, which ain't nothin' ag'inst my judgment nor yours. When Silas says, 'The girl opened her valise, took our her purse, closed her valise, opened her purse, took out a dime, closed her purse, opened her valise, put in her purse, closed her valise, give the dime to the conductor, got a nickel in change, then opened her valise, took out her purse, closed her valise—'" Stover began to rock in his saddle, then burst into a loud guffaw, followed by his companions. "Gosh! That's awful funny!"

"Si! si!" acknowledged Carara, his white teeth showing through the gloom.

"An' it's just like a fool woman," tittered Willie. "That's sure one ridic'lous line of talk."

"Still Bill" wiped his eyes with the back of a bony hand. "I know that hull monologue by heart, but I can't never get past that spot to save my soul. Right there I bog down, complete." Again he burst into wild laughter, followed by his companions. "I don't see how folks can be so dam' funny!" he gasped.

"It's natural to 'em, like warts," said Willie; "they're born with it, the same as I was born to shoot straight with either hand, and the same as the Mex was born to throw a rope. He don't know how he does it, and neither do I. Some folks can say funny things, some can sing, like Missus Melby; some can run foot-races, like that Centipede cook—" Carara breathed an eloquent Mexican oath.

"Do you reckon he fixed that race with Humpy Joe?" inquired Stover.

"Name's Skinner," Willie observed. "It sure sounds bad."

"I'm sorry Humpy left us so sudden," said Still Bill. "We'd ought to have questioned him. If we only had proof that the race was crooked—"

"You can so gamble it was crooked," the little man averred. "Them Centipede fellers never done nothin' on the square. They got Humpy Joe, and fixed it for him to lose so they could get that talkin'-machine. That's why he pulled out."

"I'd hate to think it," said the foreman, gloomily; then after a moment, during which the only sound was that of the muffled hoof-beats: "Well, what we goin' to do about it?"

"Humph! I've laid awake nights figurin' that out. I reckon we'll just have to git another foot-racer and beat Skinner. He ain't the fastest in the world."

"That takes coin. We're broke."

"Mebbe Mr. Chapin would lend a helpin' hand."

"No chance!" said Stover, grimly. "He's sore on foot-racin'. Says it disturbs us and upsets our equalubrium."

Carara fetched a deep sigh.

"It's ver' bad t'ing, Senor. I don' feel no worse w'en my gran'mother die."

The three men loped onward through the darkness, weighted heavily with disappointment.

Affairs at the Flying Heart Ranch were not all to Jack Chapin's liking. Ever since that memorable foot-race, more than a month before, a gloom had brooded over the place which even the presence of two Smith College girls, not to mention that of Mr. Fresno, was unable to dissipate. The cowboys moped about like melancholy shades, and neglected their work to discuss the disgrace that had fallen upon them. It was a task to get any of them out in the morning, several had quit, the rest were quarrelling among themselves, and the bunk-house had already been the scene of more than one encounter, altogether too sanguinary to have originated from such a trivial cause as a foot-race. It was not exactly an auspicious atmosphere in which to entertain a houseful of college boys and girls, all unversed in the ways of the West.

The master of the ranch sought his sister Jean, to tell her frankly what was on his mind.

"See here, Sis," he began, "I don't want to cast a cloud over your little house-party, but I think you'd better keep your friends away from my men."

"Why, what is the matter?" she demanded.

"Things are at a pretty high tension just now, and the boys have had two or three rows among themselves. Yesterday Fresno tried to 'kid' Willie about The Holy City; said it was written as a coon song, and wasn't sung in good society. If he hadn't been a guest, I guess Willie would have murdered him."

"Oh, Jack! You won't let Willie murder anybody, not even Berkeley, while the people are here, will you?" coaxed Miss Chapin, anxiously.

"What made you invite Berkeley Fresno, anyhow?" was the rejoinder. "This is no gilded novelty to him. He is a Western man."

Miss Chapin numbered her reasons sagely. "In the first place—Helen. Then there had to be enough men to go around. Last and best, he is the most adorable man I ever saw at a house-party. He's an angel at breakfast, sings perfectly beautifully—you know he was on the Stanford Glee Club—"

"Humph!" Jack was unimpressed. "If you roped him for Helen Blake to brand, why have you sent for Wally Speed?"

"Well, you see, Berkeley and Helen didn't quite hit it off, and Mr. Speed is—a friend of Culver's." Miss Chapin blushed prettily.

"Oh, I see! I thought myself that this affair had something to do with you and Culver Covington, but I didn't know it had lapsed into a sort of matrimonial round-up. Suppose Miss Blake shouldn't care for Speed after he gets here?"

"Oh, but she will! That's where Berkeley Fresno comes in. When two men begin to fight for her, she'll have to begin to form a preference, and I'm sure it will be for Wally Speed. Don't you see?"

The brother looked at his sister shrewdly. "It seems to me you learned a lot at Smith."

Jean tossed her head. "How absurd! That sort of knowledge is perfectly natural for a girl to have." Then she teased: "But you admit that my selection of a chaperon was excellent, don't you, Jack?"

"Mrs. Keap and I are the best of friends," Jack averred, with supreme dignity. "I'm not in the market, and a man doesn't marry a widow, anyhow. It's too old and experienced a beginning."

"Nonsense! Roberta Keap is only twenty-three. Why, she hardly knew her husband, even! It was one of those sudden, impulsive affairs that would overwhelm any girl who hadn't seen a man for four years. And then he enlisted in the Spanish War, and was killed."

"Considerate chap!"

"Roberta, you know, is my best friend, after Helen. Do be nice to her, Jack." Miss Chapin sighed. "It is too bad the others couldn't come."

"Yes, a small house-party has its disadvantages. By-the-way, what's that gold thing on your frock?"

"It's a medal. Culver sent it to me."

"Another?"

"Yes, he won the intercollegiate championship again." Miss Chapin proudly extended the emblem on its ribbon.

"I wish to goodness Covington had been here to take Humpy Joe's place," said the young cattle-man as he turned it over. "The boys are just brokenhearted over losing that phonograph."

"I'll get him to run and win it back," Jean offered, easily. Her brother laughed. "Take my advice, Sis, and don't let Culver mix up in this game! The stakes are too high. I think that Centipede cook is a professional runner, myself, and if our boys were beaten again—well, you and mother and I would have to move out of New Mexico, that's all. No, we'd better let the memory of that defeat die out as quickly as possible. You warn Fresno not to joke about it any more, and I'll take Mrs. Keap off your hands. She may be a widow, she may even be the chaperon, but I'll do it; I will do it," promised Jack—"for my sister's sake."

CHAPTER II

Helen Blake was undeniably bored. The sultry afternoon was very long—longer even than Berkeley Fresno's autobiography, and quite as dry. It was too hot and dusty to ride, so she took refuge in the latest "best seller," and sought out a hammock on the vine-shaded gallery, where Jean Chapin was writing letters, while the disconsolate Fresno, banished, wandered at large, vaguely injured at her lack of appreciation.

Absent-mindedly, the girls dipped into the box of bonbons between them. Jean finished her correspondence and essayed conversation, but her companion's blond head was bowed over the book in her lap, and the effort met with no response. Lulled by the somniferous droning of insects and lazy echoes from afar, Miss Chapin was on the verge of slumber, when she saw her guest rapidly turn the last pages of her novel, then, with a chocolate between her teeth, read wide-eyed to the finish. Miss Blake closed the book reluctantly, uncurled slowly, then stared out through the dancing heat-waves, her blue eyes shadowed with romance.

"Did she marry him?" queried Jean.

"No, no!" Helen Blake sighed, blissfully. "It was infinitely finer. She killed herself."

"I like to see them get married."

"Naturally. You are at that stage. But I think suicide is more glorious, in many cases."

Miss Chapin yawned openly. "Speaking of suicides, isn't this ranch the deadest place?"

"Oh, I don't think so at all." Miss Blake picked her way fastidiously through the bonbons, nibbling tentatively at several before making her choice. "Oh yes, you do, and you needn't be polite just because you're a guest." "Well, then, to be as truthful as a boarder, it is a little dull. Not for our chaperon, though. The time doesn't seem to drag on her hands. Jack certainly is making it pleasant for her."

"If you call taking her out to watch a lot of bellowing calves get branded, entertainment," Miss Chapin sighed.

"I wonder what makes widows so fascinating?" observed the youthful Miss Blake.

"I hope I never find out." Jean clutched nervously at the gold medal on her dress. "Wouldn't that be dreadful!"

"My dear, Culver seems perfectly healthy. Why worry?"

"I—I wish he were here."

Miss Blake leaned forward and read the inscription on her companion's medal. "Oh, isn't it heavy!" feeling it reverently.

"Pure gold, like himself! You should have seen him when he won it. Why, at the finish of that race all the men but Culver were making the most horrible faces. They were simply dead."

Miss Blake's hands were clasped in her lap. "They all make faces," said she. "Have you told Roberta about your engagement?"

"No, she doesn't dream of it, and I don't want her to know. I'm so afraid she'll think, now that mother has gone, that I asked her here just as a chaperon. Perhaps I'll tell her when Culver comes."

"I adore athletes. I wouldn't give a cent for a man who wasn't athletic."

"Does Mr. Speed go in for that sort of thing?"

"Rather! The day we met at the Yale games he had medals all over him, and that night at the dance he used the most wonderful athletic language—we could scarcely understand him. Mr. Covington must have told you all about him; they are chums, you know."

Miss Chapin furrowed her brows meditatively.

"I have heard Culver speak of him, but never as an athlete. Have you and Mr. Speed settled things between you, Helen? I mean, has he—said anything?"

Miss Blake flushed.

"Not exactly." She adjusted a cushion to cover her confusion, then leaned back complacently. "But he has stuttered dangerously several times."

A musical tinkle of silver spurs sounded in the distance, and around the corner of the cook-house opposite came Carara, the Mexican, his wide, spangled sombrero tipped rakishly over one ear, a corn-husk cigarette drooping from his lips. Evidently his presence was inspired by some special motive, for he glanced sharply about, and failing to detect the two girls behind the distant screen of vines, removed his cigarette and whistled thrice, like a quail, then, leaning against the adobe wall, curled his black silken mustaches to needle-points.

"It's that romantic Spaniard!" whispered Helen. "What does he want?"

"It's his afternoon call on Mariedetta, the maid," said Jean. "They meet there twice a day, morning and afternoon."

"A lovers' tryst!" breathed Miss Blake, eagerly. "Isn't he graceful and picturesque! Can we watch them?"

"'Sh-h! There she comes!"

From the opposite direction appeared a slim, swarthy Mexican girl, an Indian water-jug balanced upon her shoulders. She was clad in the straight-hanging native garment, belted in with a sash; her feet were in sandals, and she moved as silently as a shadow.

During the four days since Miss Blake's arrival at the Flying Heart Ranch she had seen Mariedetta flitting noiselessly here and there, but had never heard her speak. The pretty, expressionless face beneath its straight black hair had ever retained its wooden stolidity, the velvety eyes had not laughed nor frowned nor sparkled. She seemed to be merely a part of this far southwestern picture; a bit of inanimate yet breathing local color. Now, however, the girl dropped her jug, and with a low cry glided to her lover, who tossed aside his cigarette and took her in his arms. From this distance their words were indistinguishable.

"How perfectly romantic," said the Eastern girl, breathlessly. "I had no idea Mariedetta could love anybody."

"She is a volcano," Jean answered.

"Why, it's like a play!"

"And it goes on all the time."

"How gentle and sweet he is! I think he is charming. He is not at all like the other cowboys, is he?"

While the two witnesses of the scene were eagerly discussing it, Joy, the Chinese cook, emerged from the kitchen bearing a bucket of water, his presence hidden from the lovers by the corner of the building. Carara languidly released his inamorata from his embrace and lounged out of sight around the building, pausing at the farther corner to waft her a graceful kiss from the ends of his fingers, as with a farewell flash of his white teeth he disappeared. Mariedetta recovered her water-jug and glided onward into the court in front of the cookhouse, her face masklike, her movements deliberate as usual. Joy, spying the girl, grinned at her. She tossed her head coquettishly and her step slackened, whereupon the cook, with a sly glance around, tapped her gently on the arm, and said:

"Nice l'il gally."

"The idea!" indignantly exclaimed Miss Blake from her hammock.

But Mariedetta was not offended. Instead she smiled over her shoulder as she had smiled at her lover an instant before.

"Me like you fine. You like pie?" Joy nodded toward the door to the culinary department, as if to make free of his hospitality, at the instant that Carara, who had circled the building, came into view from the opposite side, a fresh cigarette between his lips. His languor vanished at the first glimpse of the scene, and he strode toward the white-clad Celestial, who dove through the open door like a prairie dog into its hole. Carara followed at his heels.

"It serves him right!" cried Miss Blake, rising. "I hope Mr. Carara—"

A din of falling pots and pans issued from the cook-house, mingled with shrill cries and soft Spanish imprecations; then, with one long-drawn wail, the pandemonium ceased as suddenly as it had commenced, and Carara issued forth, black with anger.

"Ha!" said he, scowling at Mariedetta, who had retreated, her hand upon her bosom. He exhaled a lungful of cigarette smoke through his nostrils fiercely. "You play wit' me, eh?"

"No! no!" Mariedetta ran to him, and, seizing his arm, cooed amorously in Spanish.

"Bah! Vamos!" Carara flung her from him, and stalked away.

"Well, of all the outrageous things!" said Miss Blake. "Why, she was actually flirting with that Chinaman."

"Mariedetta flirts with every man she can find," said Jean, calmly, "but she doesn't mean any harm. She'll marry Carara some time—if he doesn't kill her."

"Kill her!" Miss Blake's eyes were round. "He wouldn't do that!"

"Indeed, yes. He is a Mexican, and he has a terrible temper."

Miss Blake sank back into the hammock. "How perfectly dreadful! And yet—it must be heavenly to love a man who would kill you."

Miss Chapin lost herself in meditation for an instant. "Culver is almost like that when he is angry. Hello, here comes our foreman!"

Stover, a tall, gangling cattle-man with drooping grizzled mustache, came shambling up to the steps. His weather-beaten chaps were much too short for his lengthy limbs, the collar of his faded flannel shirt lacked an inch of meeting at the throat, its sleeves were shrunken until his hairy hands hung down like tassels. He was loose and spineless, his movements tempered with the slothfulness of the far Southwest. His appearance gave one the impression that ready-made garments are never long enough. He dusted his boots with his sombrero and cleared his throat.

"'Evening, Miss Jean. Is Mr. Chapin around?"

"I think you'll find him down by the spring-house. Can I do anything for you?"

"Nope!" Stover sighed heavily, and got his frame gradually into motion again.

"You're not looking well, Stover. Are you ill?" inquired Miss Chapin.

"Not physical," said the foreman, checking the movement which had not yet communicated itself the entire length of his frame. "I reckon my sperret's broke, that's all."

"Haven't you recovered from that foot-race?"

"I have not, and I never will, so long as that ornery Centipede outfit has got it on us."

"Nonsense, Stover!"

"What have they done?" inquired Miss Blake, curiously. "I haven't heard about any foot-race."

"You tell her," said the man, with another sigh, and a hopeless gesture that told the depth of his feelings.

"Why, Stover hired a fellow a couple of months ago as a horse-wrangler. The man said he was hungry, and made a good impression, so we put him on."

Here Stover slowly raised one booted foot and kicked his other calf. "The boys nicknamed him Humpy Joe—"

"Why, poor thing! Was he humpbacked?" inquired Helen.

"No," answered Still Bill. "Humpback is lucky. We called him Humpy Joe because when it came to running he could sure get up and hump himself."

"Soon after Joseph went to work," Jean continued, "the Centipede outfit hired a new cook. You know the Centipede Ranch—the one you see over yonder by the foot-hills."

"It wasn't 'soon after,' it was simuletaneous," said Stover, darkly. "We're beginnin' to see plain at last." He went on as if to air the injury that was gnawing him. "One day we hear that this grub-slinger over yonder thinks he can run, which same is as welcome to us as the smell of flowers on a spring breeze, for Humpy Joe had amused us in his idle hours by running jack-rabbits to earth—"

"Not really?" said Miss Blake.

"Well, no, but from what we see we judge he'd ought to limp a hundred yards in about nothing and three-fifths seconds, so we frame a race between him and the Centipede cook."

"As a matter of fact, there has been a feud for years between the two outfits," Jean offered.

"With tumulchous joy we bet our wages and all the loose gear we have, and in a burst of childish enthusiasm we put up—the talking-machine."

"A phonograph?"

"Yes. An Echo Phonograph," said Miss Chapin.

"Of New York and Paris," added Stover.

"Our boys won it from this very Centipede outfit at a bronco-busting tournament in Cheyenne."

"Wyoming." Stover made the location definite.

"The Centipede crowd took their defeat badly on Frontier Day, and swore to get even."

"And was Humpy Joe defeated?" asked Helen.

"Was he?" Still Bill shook his head sadly, and sighed for a third time. "It looked like he was running backward, miss."

"But really he was only beaten a foot. It was a wonderful race. I saw it," said Jean. "It made me think of the races at college."

Miss Blake puckered her brows trying to think.

"Joseph," she said. "No, I don't think I have seen him."

Stover's lips met grimly. "I don't reckon you have, miss. Since that race he has been hard to descry. He passed from view hurriedly, so to speak, headed toward the foot-hills, and leaping from crag to crag like the hardy shamrock of the Swiss Yelps."

Miss Blake giggled. "What made him hurry so?"

"Us!" Stover gazed at her solemnly. "We ain't none of us been the same since that foot-race. You see, it ain't the financial value of that Echo Phonograph, nor the 'double-cross' that hurts: it's the fact that the mangiest outfit in the Territory has trimmed us out of the one thing that stands for honor and excellence and 'scientific attainment,' as the judge said when we won it. That talking-machine meant more to us than you Eastern folks can understand, I reckon."

"If I were you I would cheer up," said Miss Blake, kindly, and with some importance. "Miss Chapin has a college friend coming this week, and he can win back your trophy."

Stover glanced up at Jean quickly.

"Is that right, Miss Chapin?"

"He can if he will," Jean asserted.

"Can he run?"

"He is the intercollegiate champion," declared that young lady, with proud dignity.

"And do you reckon he'd run for us and the Echo Phonograph of New York and Paris, if we framed a race? It's an honor!"

But Miss Chapin suddenly recalled her brother's caution of the day before, and hesitated.

"I—I don't think he would. You see, he is an amateur—he might be out of training—"

"The idea!" exclaimed Miss Blake, indignantly. "If Culver won't run, I know who will!" She closed her lips firmly, and turned to the foreman. "You tell your friends that we'll see you get your trophy back."

"Helen, I—"

"I mean it!" declared Miss Blake, with spirit.

Stover bowed loosely. "Thank you, miss. The very thought of it will cheer up the gang. Life 'round here is blacker 'n a spade flush. I think I'll tell Willie." He shambled rapidly off around the house.

"Helen dear, I don't want Culver to get mixed up in this affair," explained Miss Chapin, as soon as they were alone. "It's all utterly foolish. Jack doesn't want him to, either."

"Very well. If Culver doesn't feel that he can beat that cook running, I know who will try. Mr. Speed will do anything I ask. It's a shame the way those men have been treated."

"But Mr. Speed isn't a sprinter."

"Indeed!" Miss Blake bridled. "Perhaps Culver Covington isn't the only athlete in Yale College. I happen to know what I'm talking about. Naturally the two boys have never competed against each other, because they are friends—Mr. Speed isn't the sort to race his room-mate. Oh! he wouldn't tell me he could run if it were not true."

"I don't think he will consent when he learns the truth."

"I assure you," said Miss Blake, sweetly, "he will be delighted."

CHAPTER III

It was still early in the afternoon when Jack Chapin and the youthful chaperon found the other young people together on the gallery.

"Here's a telegram from Speed," began Jack.

"It's terribly funny," said Mrs. Keap. "That Mexican brought it to us down at the spring-house."

Miss Blake lost her bored expression, and sat up in the hammock.

"'Mr. Jack Chapin,'" read the owner of the Flying Heart Ranch. "'Dear Jack: I couldn't wait for Covington, so meet with brass-band and fireworks this afternoon. Have flowers in bloom in the little park beside the depot, and see that the daisies nod to me.—J. Wallingford Speed.'"

"Park, eh?" said Fresno, dryly. "Telegraph office, water-tank, and a cattle-chute. Where does this fellow think he is?"

"Here is a postscript," added Chapin.

"'I have a valet who does not seem to enjoy the trip. Divide a kiss among the girls.'"

"Well, well! He's stingy with his kisses," observed Berkeley. "Who is this humorous party?"

"He was a Freshman at Yale the year I graduated," explained Jack.

"Too bad he never got out of that class." It was evident that Mr. Speed's levity made no impression upon the Glee Club tenor. "He hates to talk about himself, doesn't he?"

"I think he is very clever," said Miss Blake, warmly.

"How well do you know him?"

"Not as well as I'd like to."

Fresno puffed at his little pipe without remarking at this.

"Well, who wants to go and meet him?" queried Jack.

"Won't you?" asked his sister.

"I can't. I've just got word from the Eleven X that I'm wanted. The foreman is hurt. I may not be back for some time."

"Nigger Mike met me," observed Fresno, darkly.

"Then Nigger Mike for Speed," laughed the cattle-man. "I've told Carara to hitch up the pintos for me. I must be going."

"I'll see that you are safely started," said the young widow; and leaving the trio on the gallery, they entered the house.

When they had gone, Jean smiled wisely at Helen. "Roberta's such a thoughtful chaperon," she observed, whereupon Miss Blake giggled.

As for Mrs. Keap, she was inquiring of Jack with genuine solicitude:

"Do you really mean that you may be gone for some time?"

"I do. It may be a week; it may be longer; I can't tell until I get over there."

"I'm sorry." Mrs. Keap's face showed some disappointment.

"So am I."

"I shall have to look out for these young people all by myself."

"What a queer little way you have of talking, as if you were years and years old."

"I do feel as if I were. I—I—well, I have had an unhappy experience. You know unhappiness builds months into years."

"When Jean got up this house-party," young Chapin began, absently, "I thought I should be bored to death. But—I haven't been. You know, I don't want to go over there?" He nodded vaguely toward the south.

"I thought perhaps it suited your convenience." His companion watched him gravely. "Are you quite sure that your sister's guests have not—had something to do with this sudden determination?"

"I am quite sure. I never liked the old Flying Heart so much as I do to-day. I never regretted leaving it so much as I do at this moment."

"We may be gone before you return."

Young Chapin started. "You don't mean that, really?" Mrs. Keap nodded her dark head. "It was all very well for me to chaperon Helen on the way out from the East, but—it isn't exactly regular for me to play that part here with other young people to look after."

"But you understand, of course—Jean must have explained to you. Mother was called away suddenly, and she can't get back now. You surely won't leave—you can't." Chapin added, hopefully: "Why, you would break up Jean's party. You see, there's nobody around here to take your place."

"But—"

"Nonsense! This is an unconventional country. What's wrong with you as a chaperon, anyway? Nobody out here even knows what a chaperon is. And I'll be back as soon as I can."

"Do you really think that would help?" Roberta's eyes laughed humorously.

"I'm not thinking of the others, I'm thinking of myself," declared the young man, boldly. "I don't want you to go before I return. You must not! If you go, I—I shall follow you." He grasped her hand impulsively.

"Oh!" exclaimed the chaperon. "This makes it even more impossible. Go! Go!" She pushed him away, her color surging. "Go to your old Eleven X Ranch right away."

"But I mean it," he declared, earnestly. Then, as she retreated farther: "It's no use, I sha'n't go now until—"

"You have known me less than a week!"

"That is long enough. Roberta—"

Mrs. Keap spoke with honest embarrassment. "Listen! Don't you see what a situation this is? If Jean and Helen should ever discover—"

"Jean planned it all; even this."

Mrs. Keap stared at him in horrified silence.

"You do love me, Roberta?" Chapin undertook to remove the girl's hands from her face, when a slight cough in the hall behind caused him to turn suddenly in time to see Berkeley Fresno passing the open door.

"There! You see!" Mrs. Keap's face was tragic. "You see!" She turned and fled, leaving the master of the ranch in the middle of the floor, bewildered, but a bit inclined to be happy. A moment later the plump face of Berkeley Fresno appeared cautiously around the door-jamb. He coughed again gravely.

"I happened to be passing," said he. "You'll pardon me?"

"This is the most thickly settled spot in New Mexico!" Chapin declared, with an artificial laugh, choking his indignation.

Fresno slowly brought his round body out from concealment.

"I came in to get a match."

"Why don't you carry matches?"

Fresno puffed complacently upon his pipe. "This," he mused, as his host departed, "eliminates the chaperon, and that helps some."

Still Bill Stover lost no time in breaking the news to the boys.

"There's something comin' off," he advised Willie. "We've got another foot-runner!"

If he had hoped for an outburst of rapture on the part of the little gun man he was disappointed, for Willie shifted his holster, smiled evilly through his glasses, and inquired, with ominous restraint:

"Where is he?"

Being the one man on the Flying Heart who had occasion to wear a gun, Willie seldom smiled from a sense of humor. Here it may be said that, deceived at first by his scholarly appearance, his fellow-laborers had jibed at Willie's affectation of a swinging holster, but the custom had languished abruptly. When it became known who he was, the other ranch-hands had volubly declared that this was a free country, where a man might exercise a wide discretion in the choice of personal adornment; and as for them, they avowed unanimously that the practice of packing a Colts was one which met with their most cordial approbation. In time Willie's six-shooter had become accepted as a part of the local scenery, and, like the scenery, no one thought of remarking upon it, least of all those who best knew his lack of humor. He had come to them out of the Nowhere, some four years previously, and while he never spoke of himself, and discouraged reminiscence in others, it became known through those vague uncharted channels by which news travels on the frontier, that back in the Texas Panhandle there was a limping marshal who felt regrets at mention of his name, and that farther north were other men who had a superstitious dread of undersized cow-men with spectacles. There were also stories of lonesome "run-ins," which, owing to Willie's secretiveness and the permanent silence of the other participants, never became more than intangible rumors. But he was a good ranchman, attended to his business, and the sheriff's office was remote, so Willie had worked on unmolested.

"This here is a real foot-runner," said Stover.

"Exactly," agreed the other. "Where is he?"

"He'll be here this afternoon. Nigger Mike's bringin' him over from the railroad. He's a guest."

"Oh!"

"Yep! He's intercollegit champeen of Yale."

"Yale?" repeated the near-sighted man. "Don't know's I ever been there. Much of a town?"

"I ain't never travelled East myself, but Miss Jean and the little yaller-haired girl say he's the fastest man in the world. I figgered we might rib up something with the Centipede." Still Bill winked sagely.

"See here, do you reckon he'd run?"

"Sure! He's a friend of the boss. And he'll run on the level, too. He can't be nothin' like Humpy."

"If he is, I'll git him," said the cowboy. "Oh, I'll git him sure, guest or no guest. But how about the phonograph?"

"The Centipede will put it up quick enough; there ain't no sentiment in that outfit."

"Then it sounds good."

"An' it'll work. Gallagher's anxious to trim us again. Some folks can't stand prosperity."

Willie spat unerringly at a grasshopper. "Lord!" said he, "it's too good! It don't sound possible."

"Well, it is, and our man will be here this evenin'. Watch out for Nigger Mike, and when he drives up let's give this party a welcome that'll warm his heart on the jump. There's nothin' like a good impression."

"I'll be on the job," assured Willie. "But I state right here and now, if we do get a race there ain't a-goin' to be no chance of our losin' for a second time."

And Stover went on his way to spread the tidings.

It was growing dark when the rattle of wheels outside the ranch-house brought the occupants to the porch in time to see Nigger Mike halt his buck-board and two figures prepare to descend.

"It's Mr. Speed!" cried Miss Blake. Then she uttered a scream as the velvet darkness was rent by a dozen tongues of flame, while a shrill yelping arose, as of an Apache war-party.

"It's the boys," said Jean. "What on earth has possessed them?"

But Stover had planned no ordinary reception, and the pandemonium did not cease until the men had emptied their weapons.

Then Mr. J. Wallingford Speed came stumbling up the steps and into the arms of his friends, the tails of his dust-coat streaming.

"Really? This is more than I expected," he gasped; then turning, doffed his straw hat to the half-revealed figures beyond the light, and cried, gayly: "Thank you, gentlemen! Thank you for missing me!"

"Yow — ee!" responded the cowboys.

"How do you do, Miss Chapin!" Speed shook hands with his hostess, and in the radiance from the open doorway she saw that his face was round and boyish, and his smile peculiarly engaging.

She welcomed him appropriately; then said: "This reception is quite as startling to us as to you. You know, Mr. Speed, that we have with us a friend of yours." She slightly drew Helen forward. "And this is Mrs. Keap, who is looking after us a bit while mother is away. Roberta, may I present Mr. Covington's friend, and ask you to be good to him?"

"Don't forget me," said Fresno, pushing into the light.

"Mr. Berkeley Fresno, of Leland Stanford University."

"Hello, Frez!" Speed thrust out his hand warmly. Not so the Californian. He replied, with hauteur:

"Fresno! F-r-e-s-n-o"; and allowed the new-comer to grasp a limp, moist hand.

"Ah! Go to the head of the class! I'm sorry you broke your wrist, however." The Eastern lad spoke lightly, and gave the palm a hearty squeeze, then turned to Jean.

"I dare say you are all disappointed, Miss Chapin, that Culver didn't come with me, but he'll be along in a day or so. I simply couldn't wait." He avoided glancing at Helen Blake, whose answering blush was lost in the darkness.

"I did think when you drove up that might be Mr. Covington with you," Miss Chapin remarked, wistfully.

"Oh no, that's my man." Speed glanced around him. "And, by-the-way, where is he?"

The sound of angry voices came through the gloom, then out into the light came Still Bill Stover, Willie, and Carara, dragging between them a globular person who was rebelling loudly.

"Stover, what is this?" questioned Miss Chapin, stepping to the edge of the veranda.

"This gent stampedes in the midst of our welcome," explained the foreman, "so we have to rope him before he gets away." It was seen now that Carara's lariat was tightly drawn about the new arrival's waist.

Then the valet broke into coherent speech, but he spoke a tongue not common to his profession.

"Nix on that welcome stuff," he burst forth, in husky, alcoholic accents; "that goes on the door-mat!" It was plain that he was very angry. "If that racket means welcome, I don't want it. Take that clothes-line off of me." Carara loosened the noose, and his captive rolled up the steps mopping his face with his handkerchief.

"What made you run away?" demanded Speed.

"Any time a bunch of bandits unhitch their gats, I'm on my way," sputtered the fat man. "I'm gun-shy, see? And when this hold-up comes off I beat it till that Cuban rummy with the medals on his dicer rides a live horse up my back."

"You don't appreciate the honor," explained his employer; then turning to the others, he announced: "Will you allow me to introduce

Mr. Lawrence Glass? He isn't really a valet, you know, Miss Chapin, and he doesn't care for the West yet. It is his first trip."

"I have heard my brother speak of Larry Glass," said Jean, graciously.

Mr. Glass courtesied awkwardly, and swinging his right foot back of his left, tapped the floor with his toe. "You were a trainer at Yale when Jack was there?"

"That's me," Mr. Glass wheezed. "I'm there with the big rub, too. Wally said he was going to train during vacation, so he staked me to a trip out here, and I came along to look after him."

"Come into the house," said Jean. "Stover will see to your baggage."

As they entered, Mr. Berkeley Fresno saw the late arrival bend over Helen Blake, and heard him murmur:

"The same unforgettable eyes of Italian blue."

And Mr. Fresno decided to dislike Wally Speed, even if it required an effort.

CHAPTER IV

It was on the following morning that Miss Blake made bold to request her favor from J. Wallingford Speed. They had succeeded in isolating themselves upon the vine-shaded gallery at the rear of the house, and the conversation had been largely of athletics, but this, judging from the rapt expression of the girl, was a subject of surpassing interest. Speed, quick to take a cue, plunged on.

"I would have made the Varsity basket-ball team myself if I hadn't been so tiny," said Helen. "I have always wanted to be tall, like Roberta."

"I shouldn't care for that," said the young man.

"You know she was a wonderful player?"

"So I've heard."

"Do you know," mused Helen, "I have never forgotten what you told me that first day we met. I think it was perfectly lovely of you."

"What was that?" Now it must be admitted that J. Wallingford Speed, in his relations with the other sex, frequently found himself in a position requiring mental gymnastics of a high order; but, as a rule, his memory was good, and he seldom crossed his own trail, so to speak. In this instance he was utterly without remembrance, however, and hence was non-committal.

"What you told me about your friendship for Mr. Covington. I think it is very unselfish of you."

"Oh, I wouldn't say that," ventured the young man, vainly racking his brain. "Nobody could help liking Culver."

"Yes; but how many men would step aside and let their best friend win prize after prize and never undertake to compete against him?" Speed blushed faintly, as any modest man might have done.

"Did I tell you that?" he inquired.

"Indeed you did."

"Then please don't speak of it to a mortal soul. I must have said a great deal that first day, but—"

"But I have spoken of it, and I said I thought it was fine of you."

"You have spoken of it?"

"Yes; I told Jean."

The Yale man undertook to change the conversation abruptly, but Miss Blake was a determined young lady. She continued:

"Of course, it was very magnanimous of you to always step aside in favor of your best friend; but it isn't fair to yourself—it really isn't. And so I have arranged a little plan whereby you can do something to prove your prowess, and still not interfere with Mr. Covington in the least."

Speed cleared his throat nervously. "Tell me," he said, "what it is."

And Miss Blake told him the story of the shocking treachery of Humpy Joe, together with the miserable undoing of the Flying Heart. "Why, those poor fellows are broken-hearted," she concluded. "Their despair over losing that talking-machine would be funny if it were not so tragic. I told them you would win it back for them. And you will, won't you? Please!" She turned her blue eyes upon him appealingly, and the young man was lost.

"I'll take ten chances," he said. "Where does the raffle come off?"

"Oh, it isn't a raffle, it's a foot-race. You must run with that Centipede cook."

"I! Run a race!" exclaimed the young college man, aghast.

"Yes, I've promised that you would. You see, this isn't like a college event, and Culver isn't here yet."

"But he'll be here in a day or so." Speed felt as if a very large man were choking him; he decided his collar was too tight.

"Oh, I've talked it all over with Jean. She doesn't want Culver to run, anyhow."

"Why not?" inquired he, suspiciously.

"I don't know, I'm sure."

"If Miss Chapin doesn't want Culver to run, you surely wouldn't want me to."

"Not at all. If Mr. Covington knew the facts of the case, he would be only too happy to do it. And, you see, you know the facts."

Speed was about to shape a gracious but firm refusal of the proffered honor when Still Bill Stover appeared at the steps, doffed his faded Stetson, and bowed limply.

"Mornin', Miss Blake." To the rear Speed saw three other men—an Indian, tall, swart, and saturnine, who walked with a limp; a picturesque Mexican with a spangled hat and silver spurs, evidently the captor of Lawrence Glass on the evening previous; and an undersized little man with thick-rimmed spectacles and a heavy-hanging holster from which peeped a gun-butt. All were smiling pleasantly, and seemed a bit abashed.

"Good-morning, Mr. Stover," said Helen, pleasantly. "This is Mr. Speed, of whom I spoke to you yesterday." Stover bowed again and mumbled something about the honor of this meeting, and Miss Blake cast her eyes over the other members of the group, saying, graciously: "I'm afraid I can't introduce your friends; I haven't met them."

The loquacious foreman came promptly to the rescue, rejoicing in an opportunity of displaying his oratorical gifts.

"Then I'll make you acquainted with the best brandin' outfit in these parts." He waved a long, bony arm at the Mexican, who flashed his white teeth. "This Greaser is Aurelio Maria Carara. Need I say he's Mex, and a preemeer roper?" Carara bowed, and swept the ground with his high-peaked head-piece. "The Maduro gent yonder is Mr. Cloudy. His mother being a Navajo squaw, named him, accordin' to the rights and customs of her tribe, selecting the title of Cloudy-but-the-Sun-Shines, which same has proved a misnomer, him bein' a pessimist for fair."

Miss Blake and her companion smiled and nodded, at which Stover, encouraged beyond measure, elaborated.

"He's had a hist'ry, too. When he reaches man's real-estate the Injun agent ropes, throws, and hog-ties him, then sends him East to be cultivated. He spends four years kickin' a football—" Speed interrupted, with an exclamation of genuine interest.

"Oh, it's true as gospel," the foreman averred. "When he goes lame in his off leg they ship him back, and in spite of them handicaps he has become one rustlin' savage at a round-up."

"What college did you attend?" inquired Speed, politely. The question fell upon unresponsive ears. Cloudy did not stir nor alter the direction of his sombre glance.

"He don' talk none," Stover explained. "Conversation, which I esteem as a gift deevine, is a lost art with him. I reckon he don't average a word a week. What language he did know he has forgot, and what he ain't forgot he distrusts."

Turning to the near-sighted man who had been staring at the college youth meanwhile, the spokesman took a deep breath, and said, simply yet proudly, as if describing the piece de resistance of this exhibition:

"The four-eyed gent is Willie, plain Willie, a born range-rider, and the best hip shot this side of the Santa Fe trail!"

Speed beheld an undersized man of indeterminate age, hollow-chested, thin-faced, gravely benignant. It was not alone his glasses that lent him a scholarly appearance; he had the stooped shoulders, the thoughtful intensity of gaze, the gentle, hesitating backwardness of a book-raised man. There were tutors at Yale quite as colorless, characterless and indefinite, and immensely more forceful. In place of the revolver at his belt, it seemed as if Willie should have carried a geologist's pick, a butterfly-net, or a magnifying-glass: one was prepared to hear him speak learnedly of microscopy, or even, perhaps, of settlement work. As a cowboy he was utterly out of place, and it was quite impossible to take Stover's words seriously. Nevertheless, Speed acknowledged the introduction pleasantly, while the benevolent little man blinked back of his lenses. Stover addressed himself to Miss Blake.

"I told the boys what you said, miss, and we four has come as a delegation to find out if it goes."

"Mr. Speed and I were just talking about it when you came," said Helen. "I'm sure he will consent if you add your entreaties to mine."

"It would sure be a favor," said the cow-man, at which the others drew nearer, as if hanging on Speed's answer. Even Cloudy turned his black eyes upon the young man.

The object of their co-operate gaze shifted his feet uncomfortably and felt minded to flee, but the situation would not permit of it. Besides, the affair interested him. His mind was working rapidly, albeit his words were hesitating.

"I — I'm afraid I'm not in shape to run," he ventured. But Stover would have none of this modesty, admirable as it might appear.

"Oh, I talked with your trainer just now. I told him you was tipped off to us as a sprinter."

"What did he say?" inquired Speed, with alarm.

"He said 'no' at first, till I told him who let it out; then he laughed, and said he guessed you was a runner, but you didn't work at it regular. I asked him how good you was, and he said none of the college teams would let you run. That's good enough for us, Mr. Speed."

"But I'm not in condition," objected the youth, with a sigh of gratitude at Glass's irony.

"I reckon he knows more about that than you do. We covered that point too, and Mr. Glass said you was never better than you are right now. Anyhow, you don't have to bust no records to beat this cook. He ain't so fast."

"It would sure be a kind-hearted act if you'd do it for us," said the little man in his high, boyish voice. It was a shock to discover that he spoke in a dialect. "There's a heap of sentiment connected with this affair. You see, outside of being a prize that we won at considerable risk, there goes with this phonograph a set of records, among which we all have our special favorites. Have you ever heard Madam-o-sella Melby sing The Holy City?"

"I didn't know she sang it," said Speed.

"Take it from me, she did, and you've missed a heap."

"You bet," Stover agreed, in a hushed, awed tone.

"Well, you must have heard Missus Heleney Moray in The Baggage Coach Ahead?" queried the scholarly little man. At mention of his beloved classic, Carara, the Mexican, murmured, softly:

"Ah! The Baggage Car — Te'adora Mora! God bless 'er!"

"I must confess I've never had the pleasure," said Speed, whereupon the speaker regarded him pityingly, and Stover, jealous that so much of the conversation had escaped him, inquired:

"Can it be that you never heard that monologue, Silas on Fifth Avenoo?"

Again Speed shook his head.

As if the very memory were hilariously funny, Still Bill's shoulders heaved, and stifled laughter caused his Adam's apple to race up and down his leathern throat. Swallowing his merriment at length, he recited, in a choking voice, as follows: "Silas goes up Fifth Avenoo and climbs into a bus. There is a girl settin' opposite. He says, 'The girl opened her valise, took out her purse, closed her valise, opened her purse, took out a dime, closed her purse, opened her valise, put in her purse, closed her valise, handed the dime to the conductor, got a nickle in change, opened her valise, took out her purse, closed her valise, opened her purse—'"

At this point the speaker fell into ungovernable hysteria and exploded, rocking back and forth, slapping his thighs and hiccoughing with enjoyment. Willie followed him, as did Carara. Even Cloudy showed his teeth, and the two young people on the porch found themselves joining in from infection. It was patent that here lay some subtle humor sufficient to convulse the Far Western nature beyond all reason; for Stover essayed repeatedly to check his laughter before gasping, finally: "Gosh 'lmighty! I never can get past that place. He! He! He! Whoo-hoo! That's sure ridic'lous, for fair." He wiped his eyes with the back of a sun-browned hand, and his frame was racked with barking coughs. "I know the whole blame thing by heart, but—I can't recite it to you. I bog down right there. Seems like some folks is the darndest fools!"

Speed allowed this good-humor to banish his trepidation, and assured the foreman that Silas on Fifth Avenue must indeed be a very fine monologue.

"It's my favorite," said Still Bill, "but we all have our picks. Cloudy here likes Navajo, which I agree is attuned to please the savage year, but to my mind it ain't in the runnin' with Silas."

"You see what the phonograph means to these gentlemen," said Miss Blake. "I think it's a crying shame that they were cheated out of it, don't you?"

Speed began to outline a plan hastily in his mind.

"I assured them that you would win it back for them, and—"

"We sure hope you will," said Willie, earnestly.

"Amen!" breathed the lanky foreman, his cheeks still wet from his tears of laughter, but his face drawn into lines of eagerness.

"Please! For my sake!" urged Helen, placing a gentle little hand upon her companion's arm.

Speed closed his eyes, so to speak, and leaped in the dark.

"All right, I'll do it!"

"Yow-ee!" yelled Stover. "We knew you would!" Willie was beaming benignantly through his glasses, while both Carara and Cloudy showed their heartfelt gratitude. "Thank you, Miss Blake. Now we'll show up that shave-tail Centipede crowd for what it is."

"Wait!" Speed checked the outburst. "I'll consent upon conditions. I'll run, provided you can arrange the race for an 'unknown.'"

"What does that mean?" Helen asked.

"It means that I don't want my name known in the matter. Instead of arranging for Mr. Whatever-the-Cook's-Name-Is to run a race with J. W. Speed, he must agree to compete against a representative of the Flying Heart ranch, name unknown."

"I don't think that is fair!" cried the girl. "Think of the honor."

"Yes, but I'm an amateur. I'd lose my standing."

"That goes for us," said Stover. "We don't care what name you run under. We'll frame the race. Lordy! but this is a glorious event."

"We can't thank you enough," Willie piped. "You're a true sport, Mr. Speed, and we aim to see that you don't get the worst of it in no way. This here race is goin' to be on the square-you hear me talkin'. No double-cross this time." Unconsciously the speaker's hand strayed to the gun at his belt, while his smile was grim. Speed started.

"What day shall we set?" inquired Stover.

Wally rapidly calculated the date of Culver's arrival, and said: "A week from Saturday." Covington would soon be en route, and was due to arrive a few days thereafter.

"We'd like to make it to-morrow," ventured Willie.

"Oh, but I must have a chance to get in trim," said the college man.

"One week from Saturday goes," announced Stover, "and we thank you again." Turning to Carara, he directed: "Rope your buckskin, and hike for the Centipede. Tell 'em to unlimber their coin. I'll draw a month's wages in advance for every son-of-a-gun on the Flying Heart, and we'll arrange details to-night."

"Si," agreed Carara. "I go."

"And don't waste no time neither," directed Willie. "You tear like a jack-rabbit ahead of a hot wind."

Carara tossed his cigarette aside, and the sound of his spurs was lost around the corner of the house.

"This makes a boy of me," the last speaker continued. "I can hear the plaintiff notes of Madam-o-sella Melby once again."

CHAPTER V

Larry Glass discovered his protege on the rear porch engrossed with Miss Blake, and signalled him from afar; but the young man ignored the signal, and the trainer strolled up to the steps.

"Hello, Larry! What's on your mind?" inquired Speed.

"I'd like to see you." Glass, clad in his sportiest garments, seemed utterly lacking in the proper appreciation of a valet's position. He treated his employer with a tolerant good-nature.

Miss Blake excused herself and went into the house, whereupon her companion showed his irritation. "See here, Larry, don't you know better than to interrupt me in the midst of a hammock talk?"

"Oh, that's all right," wheezed the trainer. "As long as you didn't spill her out, she'll be back."

"Well, what is it?"

"I had a stomach-laugh slipped to me just now." He began to shake.

"So you broke up my tete-a-tete to tell me a funny story?"

"Listen here. These cowboys have got you touted for a foot-runner." This time Glass laughed aloud, hoarsely. "They have framed a race with a ginny down the block."

"All right, I'll run."

Mr. Glass's face abruptly fell into solemn lines. "Quit your kiddin', Wally; you couldn't run a hundred yards in twenty minutes. These guys are on the level. They've sent General Garcia over to cook it."

"Yes. The race comes off in ten days."

Glass allowed his mouth to drop open and his little eyes to peer forth in startled amazement.

"Then it's true? I guess this climate is too much for you," he said. "When did you feel this comin' on?"

Speed laughed. "I know what I'm doing." With an effort at restraint, the trainer inquired:

"What's the idea?"

"I'll tell you how it came up, Larry. I—I'm very fond of Miss Blake. That's why I broke the record getting out here as soon as I was invited. Well, she believes, from something I said—one of those odd moments, you know—that I'm a great athlete, and she told those cowboys that I'd gladly put on my spiked shoes and carry their colors to victory. You've heard about the phonograph?"

Glass smiled wearily. "I can't hear nothing else. The gang is daffy on grand opera."

"When I was accused of being an athlete I couldn't deny it, could I?"

"I see. You was stringin' the gal, and she called you, eh?"

"I wouldn't express it in quite those terms. I may have exaggerated my abilities slightly." Glass laughed. "She is such a great admirer of athletics, it was quite natural. Any man would have done the same. She got me committed in front of the cowboys, and I had to accept—or be a quitter."

Glass nodded appreciatively. "All the same," said he, "you've got more nerve than a burglar. How you goin' to side-step?"

"I made the match for an 'unknown.'" Speed winked. "Covington will be here in a day or two. I'll wire him to hurry up. Fortunately I brought a lot of athletic clothes with me, so I'll go into training under your direction. When Covington gets here I'll let him run."

The fat man sighed with relief. "Now I'm hep. I was afraid you'd try to go through with it."

"Hardly. I'll sprain an ankle, or something. She'll be there with the sympathy. See? Covington will run the race; the cowboys will get their phonograph; and I'll get—well, if I can beat out this Native Son tenor singer, I'll invite you to the wedding. There wasn't any other way out."

Glass mopped his brow. "You had me wingin' for a while, but I plugged your game with the cowboys. Pawnee Bill and his Congress of Rough Riders think you're a cyclone."

"It's the first chance I ever had to wear that silk running-suit. Who knows, maybe I can run!"

"Nix, now! Don't kid yourself too far. This thing is funny enough as it stands."

"Oh, I dare say it looks like a joke to you, but it doesn't to me, Larry. If I don't marry that girl, I—I'll go off my balance, that's all, and I'm not going to overlook any advantage whatever. Fresno sings love-songs, and he's got a mint of money. Well, I'm going to work this athletic pose to death. I'm going into training, I'm going to talk, eat, sleep, live athletics for a week, and when I'm unexpectedly crippled on the eve of the race, it is going to break my heart. Understand! I am going to be so desperately disappointed that I'll have to choose between suicide and marriage. The way I feel now, I think I'll choose marriage. But you must help."

"Leave it to me, Bo!"

"In the first place, I want some training-quarters."

"That's right, don't be a piker."

"And I want you to boost."

"I'm there! When do we begin?"

"Right away. Unpack my running-suit and rub some dirt on it—it's too new. I think I'll limber up, and let her get a look at the clothes."

"It's a bright idea; but don't let these animal-trainers see you run, or the stuff will be cold in a minute."

"Fine! We'll have secret practice! That suits me perfectly." Speed laughed with joy.

From inside the house came the strains of Dearie, sung in a sympathetic tenor, and upon the conclusion Berkeley Fresno's voice inquiring:

"Miss Blake, did I ever tell you about the time I sang Dearie to the mayor's daughter in Walla Walla?"

Miss Blake appeared on the gallery with her musical admirer at her elbow.

"Yes," said she, sweetly. "You told me all about the mayor's daughter a week ago." Then spying Speed and his companion, she exclaimed: "Mr. Fresno has a fine voice, hasn't he? He sings with the Stanford Glee Club."

"Indeed."

"Sure!" The Native Son of the Golden West shook up a hammock-cushion for the girl. "Tenor!" said he, sententiously.

"Say no more," Speed remarked; "it's all right with us!"

Fresno looked up.

"What's wrong with my singing?"

"Oh, I've just told the girls that you're going to run that foot-race," Helen interposed, hurriedly, at which Fresno exploded.

"What's wrong with my running?" inquired Speed.

"I can beat you!"

Larry Glass nudged his employer openly, and seemed on the verge of hysteria. "Let him go," said he. "Let him go; he's funny."

Speed addressed Helen, with a magnanimous smile:

"Suppose we allow Frez to sing this foot-race? We'll pull it off in the treble cleff."

"Oh, I mean it!" maintained the tenor, stubbornly. "I don't want to run Skinner, the cook, but I'll run you to see who does meet him."

Speed shrugged his shoulders indulgently.

"I'm afraid you're a little overweight."

"I'll train down."

"Perhaps if you wait until I beat this cook, I'll take you on."

Glass broke out, in husky indignation: "Sure! Get a rep, Cull, get a rep!" Then to his employer: "Come on, Wally, you've got to warm up." He mounted the steps heavily with his protege.

When they had gone, Miss Blake clapped her hands.

"I'm so excited!" she exclaimed. "You see, it's all my doings! Oh, how I adore athletes!"

"Most young girls do," Fresno smiled, sourly. "My taste runs more to music." After a moment's meditation, he observed: "Speed doesn't look like a sprinter to me. I—I'll wager he can't do a hundred yards in fifteen-two."

"'Fifteen-two' is cribbage," said Miss Blake.

"Fifteen and two-fifths seconds is what I mean."

"Is that fast?"

Fresno smiled, indulgently this time. "Jean's friend Covington can go the distance in nine and four-fifths seconds. He's a real sprinter. I think this fellow is a joke."

"Indeed he is not! If Mr. Covington can run as fast as that, Mr. Speed can run faster. He told me so."

"Oh!" Fresno looked at her curiously. "The world's record is nine and three-fifths; that's the limit of human endurance."

"I hope he doesn't injure himself," breathed the girl, and the tenor wandered away, disgusted beyond measure. When he was out of hearing, he remarked, aloud:

"I'll bet he runs so slow we'll have to wind a stop-watch on him. Anyhow, I think I'll find out something more about this race."

Once in his room, Mr. J. Wallingford Speed made a search for writing materials, while Larry Glass overhauled a trunk filled with athletic clothing of various descriptions. There were running-suits, rowing-suits, baseball and football suits, sweaters, jerseys, and bath robes—all of which were new and unstained. At the bottom Glass discovered a box full of bronze and near-gold emblems.

"Here's your medals," said he.

"Good! I'll wear them."

"Nix! You can't do that. Those gals will get wise." He selected one, and read on the reverse side. "Clerk of the course"; another was engraved "Starter." All were official badges of some sort or other. "You always were strong on the 'Reception Committee' stuff. There's six of them," said he.

Speed pointed to the bureau. "Try a nail-file. See if you can't scratch off the lettering. How's this?" He read what he had written for the wire. "'Culver Covington, and so forth. Come quick. First train. Native Son making love to Jean.—Wally.' Ten words, and it tells the whole story. I can hardly explain why I want him, can I? He expects to stop off in Omaha for a day or two, but he'll be under way in an hour after he gets this. I hate to spoil his little visit, but he can take that in on his way home. Now I'll ring for somebody, and have this taken over to the station by the first wagon."

"Say, you better scratch this Fresno," said Larry.

"Why?"

"He's hep to you."

"Nonsense!"

Glass looked up at a sound, to discover Mariedetta, the Mexican maid, who had come in answer to Speed's call.

"In the doorway'" the trainer said, under his breath. "Pipe the Cuban Queen!"

"You call?" inquired Mariedetta of the younger man.

"Yes, I want this telegram to go to the depot as soon as possible."

Mariedetta took the message and turned silently, but as she went she flashed a look at Glass which caused that short-waisted gentleman to wink at his companion.

"Some frill! Eh? I'm for her! She's strong for me, too."

"How do you know?"

"We talked it over. I gave her a little kiss to keep for me."

"Careful, Larry! She may have a cowboy sweetheart."

Glass grunted, disparagingly.

"Them ginnys is jokes to me."

As Speed talked he clad himself in his silken uniform, donned his spiked shoes, and pinned the medals upon his chest.

"How do I look?" he queried.

"Immense! If she likes athletes, it's a walk-away for you."

"Then give me the baby-blue bath robe with the monogram. We'll go out and trot around a little."

But his complacency received a shock as he stepped out upon the veranda. Not only Helen Blake awaited him, but the other girls as well, while out in front were a dozen or more cowboys whom Fresno had rallied. "Goin' to take a little run, eh?" inquired Stover. "We allowed we'd lay off a few minutes and watch you."

"Thanks!"

"Yes," Fresno spoke up. "I told the boys we'd better hold a stop-watch on you and see what shape you're in."

"A stop-watch?" said Glass, sharply.

"Yes. I have one."

"Not to-day," said Speed's trainer. "No!" he admonished, as his protege turned upon him. "Some other time, mebbe. You're just off a long trip, and I can't risk gettin' you stove up."

"To-morrow, perhaps," urged Fresno.

"I wouldn't promise."

"Then the next day. I've timed lots of men. The watch is correct."

"Let's see it." Glass held out his hand.

"Oh, it's a good watch. It cost me one hundred and twenty-five dollars."

As Glass reached for the timepiece an unfortunate accident occurred. Speed struck his elbow, and the watch fell. Fresno dove for it, then held it to his ear and shook it.

"You've broken it!" he cried, accusingly.

"Oh, I'm sorry! My fault," Speed apologized.

"If it was your fault, maybe you'll fix it," suggested the tenor.

"Gladly!" Speed turned to his trainer. "Buy a new alarm-clock for our little friend." He stripped off his bath robe, and handed it to his trainer. "Is she looking at me?" he whispered.

"Both eyes, big as saucers."

Speed settled his spikes into the dirt as he had seen other sprinters do, set himself for an instant, then loped easily around the house and out of sight.

To the cowboys this athletic panoply was vastly impressive. With huge satisfaction they noticed the sleeveless shirt, the loose running-trunks, and, above all, the generous display of medals. With a wild yell of delight they broke out upon the trail of their champion, only to have Glass thrust his corpulent body in their path. With an upflung arm he stemmed the tide.

"It's no use, boys," he cried, "he's a mile away!"

CHAPTER VI

"This doesn't look much like our storehouse, does it?" Jean paused in her task, and, seating herself upon the summit of a step-ladder, scrutinized with satisfaction the transformation wrought by a myriad of college flags, sofa cushions, colored shawls, and bunting.

Roberta Keap dropped her hammer with an exclamation of pain.

"Ouch!" she cried, "I've hurt my thumb. I can't hit where I look when people are talking."

"Why don't you pin them up?" queried Miss Blake, sweetly. "A hammer is so dangerous."

Mrs. Keap mumbled something, but her enunciation was indistinct, owing to the fact that her thumb was in her mouth. Helen finished tying a bow of ribbon upon the leg of a stool, patted it into proper form, then said:

"It looks cheerful."

"And restful," added Jean.

"I think a gymnasium should be restful, above all things," agreed Helen. "Most of them are so bare and strenuous-looking they give one a headache." She spied a Whiteley exerciser fastened against the wall, the one bit of gymnastic apparatus in the room. 'Oh, the puller!' she cried. "I mustn't forget the puller!" She selected a pink satin ribbon, and tied a chic bow upon one of the wooden handles. "There! We can let him in now."

"Oh dear!" Jean descended from her precarious position and admitted, "I'm tired out."

All that morning the three had labored, busily transforming the store-room into training-quarters for Speed, who had declared that such things were not only customary but necessary. To be sure, it adjoined the bunk-room, where the cowboys slept, and there were no gymnastic appliances to give it character, but it was the only space available, and what it lacked in horizontal bars, dumb-bells, and Indian clubs it more than compensated for by a cosey-corner, a window-seat, and many cushions. Speed had expressed his delight with the idea, and agreed to wait for a glimpse of it.

And the atmosphere at the Flying Heart Ranch was clearing. The gloom of the cowboys had given way to a growing excitement, a part of which communicated itself to the occupants of the house. The lassitude of previous days was gone, the monotony had disappeared, and Miss Chapin had cause to rejoice at the presence of her latest guest, for Speed was like a tonic. He was everywhere, he inspired them all, laughter followed in his wake. Even in the bunk-house the cowboys retailed his extravagant stories with delight. The Flying Heart had come into its own at last; the Centipede, most scorned and hated of rivals, was due for lasting defeat. Even Cloudy, the Indian, relaxed and spoke at rare intervals, while Willie worked about the place gleefully, singing snatches of Sam Bass in a tuneless falsetto. Carara had come back from the Centipede with news that gladdened the hearts of his hearers: not only would that despicable outfit consent to run a foot-race, but they clamored for it. They did not dicker over details nor haggle about terms, but consented to put up the phonograph again, and all the money at their disposal as well. The cook was in training.

Of all the denizens of the Flying Heart but two failed to enter fully into the spirit of the thing. Berkeley Fresno looked on with a cynicism which he was too wise to display before Miss Blake. Seeing the lady of his dreams monopolized by a rival, however, inspired him to sundry activities, and he spent much of his time among the cowboys, whom he found profitable to the point of mystery.

Mrs. Keap, the youthful chaperon, seemed likewise mastered by some private trouble, and puzzled her companions vaguely. Helen reported that she did not sleep, and once Jean found her crying softly. She seemed, moreover, to be apprehensive, in a tremulous, reasonless ways but when with friendly sympathy they brought the subject up, she dismissed it. In spite of secret tears, she had lent willing hands to the decoration of the gymnasium, and now nursed her swollen thumb with surprising good nature.

"Shall we let them in?" she inquired. "We have done all we can."

"Yes; we have finished."

In a flutter of anticipation Jean and Helen put the final touches to their task, while Mrs. Keap stepped to the door and called Speed.

He came at once, followed by Larry Glass, who, upon grasping the scheme of decoration, smote his brow and balanced dizzily upon his heels. Speed was lost in admiration.

"Its wonderful!" ejaculated the young athlete. "Those college flags give it just the right touch. And see the cosey-corner!"

Glass regained his voice sufficiently to murmur, sarcastically, "Say, ain't this a swell-looking drum?"

"We've used every bit of bunting on the ranch," said Jean.

"See the Mexican shawls!" Mrs. Keap added.

"And look," cried Miss Blake, "I brought you my prayer-rug!" She displayed a small Persian rug, worn and faded, evidently a thing of great age, at which Speed uttered an exclamation. "I always carry it with me, and put it in front of my bed wherever I happen to be."

Berkeley Fresno, drawn by the irresistible magnetism of Miss Blake's presence, wandered in and ran his eyes over the room.

Speed took the rug and examined it curiously. "It's an old-timer, isn't it? Must be one of the first settlers."

"Yes. It's thousands and thousands of years old. Father picked it up somewhere in Asia."

"How does it work?" queried Glass, feeling of it gingerly.

"It's a very holy thing," Helen explained. "The Mohammedan stands on it facing the East and cries 'Allah!'"

"Alley!" repeated the trainer. "No. Allah!"

"'Allah' is the Mohammedan divinity," explained Speed.

"I've got you." Glass was greatly interested.

"Then he makes his prayer. It is such a sacred thing that when one's feet are on it no harm can come to one."

"Well, what d'you think of that?" murmured the trainer.

Fresno laughed pleasantly. "It's too bad it isn't long enough to run this footrace on."

"Do you believe in the charm?" inquired Speed of Helen.

"Of course I do," she answered.

He laughed sceptically, whereupon Larry Glass broke in with husky accents:

"Nix on the comedy! I bet it's a wizard!"

His employer gazed warmly at the owner of the priceless treasure, and, taking the rug tenderly, pressed his lips to it.

Fresno shook his head in disgust; the brazen methods of this person were unbearable.

"Why all the colors?" asked he. "You can sing best where there is a piano. I can train best under the shadow of college emblems. I am a temperamental athlete."

"You'll be a dead athlete if you don't beat this cook." The Californian was angry.

"Indeed!" exclaimed his rival, airily.

"That's what I remarked. Did they tell you what happened to Humpy Joe, your predecessor?"

"It must have been an accident, judging from his name." At which Miss Blake tittered. She was growing to enjoy these passages at arms; they thrilled her vaguely.

"The only accident connected with the affair was that Still Bill and Willie didn't have their guns."

Glass started nervously. "Did these rummies want to shoot him?" he inquired.

"Certainly," said Fresno. "He lost a foot-race."

In spite of his assurance, J. Wallingford Speed felt a tremor of anxiety, but he laughed it off, saying: "One would think a foot-race in this country was a pearl necklace."

"These cowboys ain't good losers, eh?" queried Glass.

"It's win or die out here."

During the ensuing pause Mrs. Keap took occasion to call Speed aside. "I have something to contribute to the training-quarters if you will help me bring it out," said she.

The young man bowed. "Most gladly."

"We'll be back in a little while," the chaperon announced to the others, and a moment later, when she and Speed had reached the veranda of the house, she paused.

"I—I want to speak to you," she began, hesitatingly. "It was just an excuse."

Wally looked at her with concern, for it was plain that she was deeply troubled.

"What is it?"

"I have been trying to get a word alone with you ever since I heard about this foot-race." The young man chilled with apprehension as Mrs. Keap turned her dark eyes upon him searchingly.

"Why do you want to run?"

"To win back the cowboys' treasure. My heart is touched," he declared, boldly. Mrs. Keap smiled.

"I believe the latter, but are you sure you can win?"

"Abso-blooming-lutely."

"I didn't know you were a sprinter."

Speed shrugged his shoulders.

"Have you had experience?"

"Oceans of it!"

Mrs. Keap mused for a moment. "Tell me," said she, finally, "at what intercollegiate game did you run last?"

"I didn't run last; I ran first." It was impossible to resent the boy's smile.

"Then at what game did you last run? I hope I'm not too curious?"

"Oh no, not at all!" Speed stammered.

"Or, if it is easier, at what college games did you first run?" Mrs. Keap was laughing openly now.

"Why the clear, ringing, rippling laughter?" asked the young man, to cover his confusion.

"Because I think it is very funny."

"Oh, you do!" Speed took refuge behind an attitude of unbending dignity, but the young widow would have none of it.

"I know all about you," said she. "You are a very wonderful person, of course; you are a delightful fellow at a house-party, and a most suitable individual generally, but you are not an athlete, in spite of those beautiful clothes in your trunk."

"Who told you?"

"Culver Covington."

"I didn't know you two were acquainted."

Mrs. Keap flushed. "He told me all about you long ago. You wear all the athletic clothes, you know all the talk, you have tried to make the team a dozen times, but you are not even a substitute. You are merely the Varsity cheer-leader. Culver calls you 'the head-yeller.'"

"Columbus has discovered our continent!" said Speed. "You are a very wise chaperon, and you must have a corking memory for names, but even a head-yeller is better than a glee-club quarter-back." He nodded toward the bunk-house, whence they had come. "You haven't told anybody?"

"Not yet."

"'Yet,'" he quoted. "The futurity implied in that word disturbs me. Suppose you and I keep it for a little secret? Secrets are very delightful at house-parties."

"Don't you consider your action deceitful?"

"Not at all. My motto is 'We strive to please.'"

"Think of Helen."

"That's it; I can't think of anything else! She's mad about athletics, and I had to do something to stand off this weight-lifting tenor."

"Is it any wonder a woman distrusts every man she meets?" mused the chaperon. "Helen might forgive you, I couldn't."

"Oh, it's not that bad. I know what I'm doing."

"You will cause these cowboys to lose a lot more money."

"Not at all. When Culver arrives—"

"Oh, that is what I want to talk over with you," Mrs. Keap broke in, nervously.

"Then it isn't about the foot-race? You are not angry?" Speed brightened amazingly.

"I'm not exactly angry; I'm surprised and grieved. Of course, I can't forgive deceit—I dare say I am more particular than most people."

"But you won't tell?" Mrs. Keap indicated in some subtle manner that she was not above making terms, whereupon her companion declared, warmly: "I'm yours for life! Ask me for my watch, my right eye, anything! I'll give it to you!"

"I assure you I sha'n't ask anything so important as that, but I shall ask a favor."

"Name it and it is yours!" Speed wrung the hand she offered.

"And perhaps I can do more than keep silent—although I don't see what good it will do. Perhaps I can help your suit."

"Gracious lady, all I ask is that you thrust out your foot and trip up Berkeley Fresno whenever he starts toward her. Put him out of the play, and I shall be the happiest man in the world."

"Agreed."

"Now, in what way can I serve you?"

Mrs. Keap became embarrassed, while the same shadowy trouble that had been observed of late settled upon her.

"I simply hate to ask it," she said, "but I suppose I must. There seems to be no other way out of it." Turning to him suddenly, she said, in a low, intense voice: "I—I'm in trouble, Mr. Speed, such dreadful trouble!"

"Oh, I'm so sorry!" he answered her, with genuine solicitude. "You needn't have made any conditions. I would have done anything I could for you."

"That's very kind, for I don't like our air of conspiracy, but"— Mrs. Keap was wringing her slender hands—"I just can't tell the girls. You—you can help me."

Speed allowed her time to grow calm, when she continued:

"I—I am engaged to be married."

"Felicitations!"

"Not at all," said the young widow, wretchedly. "That is the awful part of it. I am engaged to two men!" She turned her brown eyes full upon him; they were strained and tragic.

Speed felt himself impelled to laugh immoderately, but instead he observed, in a tone to relieve her anxiety:

"Nothing unusual in that; it has been done before. Even I have been prodigal with my affections. What can I do to relieve the congestion?"

"Please don't make light of it. It means so much to me. I — I'm in love with Jack Chapin."

"With Jack!"

"Yes. When I came here I thought I cared for somebody else. Why, I wanted to come here just because I knew that — that somebody else had been invited too, and we could be together."

"And he couldn't come — "

"Wait! And then, when I got here, I met Jack Chapin. That was less than a week ago, and yet in that short time I have learned that he is the only man I can ever love — the one man in all the world."

"And you can't accept because you have a previous engagement. I see! Jove! It's quite dramatic. But I don't see why you are so excited? If the other chap isn't coming — "

"But he is! That is what makes it so dreadful! If those two men should meet" — Mrs. Keap buried her face in her hands and shuddered — "there would be a tragedy, they are both so frightfully jealous." She began to tremble, and Speed laid a comforting hand upon her shoulder.

"I think you must be exciting yourself unduly," said he, "Jean's other friends didn't come. There's nobody due now but Culver Cov — "

"That's who it is!" Roberta raised her pallid face as the young man fell back.

"Culver! Great Scott! Why, he's engaged — "

"What!"

"Nothing! I — I — " Speed paused, at an utter loss for words. "You see, he'll discover the truth."

"Does he know you are here?"

"No. I intended to surprise him. I was jealous. I couldn't bear to think of his being here with other girls — men are so deceitful! That's why I consented to act as chaperon to Helen. And now to think that I should have met my fate in Jack Chapin!"

"I see. You want me to break the news to Culver."

"No! no!" Mrs. Keap was aghast. "If he even suspected the truth he'd become a raging lion. Oh, I've been quite distracted ever since Jack left!"

"Well, what am I to do? You must have some part laid out for me?"

"I have. A desperate situation demands a desperate remedy. I've lost all conscience. That's why I agreed to protect you if you'd protect me."

"Go ahead."

"Culver is your friend."

"We're closer than a chord in G."

"Then you must wire him—"

"I have—"

" —not to come."

"What!" J. Wallingford Speed started as if a wasp had stung him.

"You must wire him at once not to come. I don't care what excuse you give, but stop him. Stop him!"

Speed reached for a pillar; he felt that the porch was spinning slowly beneath his feet.

"Oh, see here, now! I can't do that!"

"You promised!" cried Mrs. Keap, fiercely. "I have tried to think of something to tell him, but I'm too frightened."

"Yes, but—but I—want him here—for this foot-race." Wally swallowed bravely.

"Foot-race!" stormed the widow, indignantly. "Would you allow an insignificant thing like a foot-race to wreck a human life? Two human lives? Three?"

"Can't you—wire him?"

Mrs. Keap stamped her foot. "If he dreamed I was here he would hire a special train. No! It must come from you. You are his best friend."

"What can I say?" demanded the bewildered Speed, unhappily. "I don't care what you say, I don't care what you do—only do something, and do it quickly before he has time to leave Chicago." Then sensing the hesitation in her companion's face: "Or perhaps you prefer to have Helen know the deceit you have practiced upon her? And I fancy these cowboys would resent the joke, don't you? What do you think would happen if they discovered their champion to be merely a cheerleader with a trunkful of new clothes, who can't do a single out-door sport— not one!"

"Wait!" Speed mopped his brow with a red-and-blue silk handkerchief. "I'll do my best."

"Then I shall do my part." And Mrs. Keap, who could not bear deception, turned and went indoors while J. Wallingford Speed, a prey to sundry misgivings, stumbled down the steps, his head in a whirl.

CHAPTER VII

Berkeley Fresno was devoting himself to Miss Blake.

"What do you think of our decorations?" she inquired.

"They are more or less athletic," he declared. "Was it Mr. Speed's idea?"

"Yes. He wanted training-quarters."

"It's a joke, isn't it?"

"I don't think so. Mr. Fresno, why do you dislike Mr. Speed?"

Fresno bent a warm glance upon the questioner. "Don't you know?"

Helen shook her head with bland innocence. "Then you do dislike him?"

"No, indeed! I like him—he makes me laugh." Helen bridled loyally. "Did you see those medals he wore yesterday?" the young man queried.

"Of course, and I thought them beautiful."

"How were they inscribed? He wouldn't let me examine them."

"Naturally. If I had trophies like that I would guard them too."

Fresno nodded, musingly. "I gave mine away."

"Oh, are you an athlete?"

"No, but I timed a foot-race once. They gave me a beautiful nearly-bronze emblem so that I could get into the infield."

"And did you win?"

"No! no! I didn't run! Don't you understand? I was an official." Fresno was vexed at the girl's lack of perception. "I'm not an athlete, Miss Blake. I'm just an ordinary sort of a chap." He led her to a seat, while Jean enlisted the aid of Larry Glass and completed the finishing touches to the decorations. "Athletics don't do a fellow any good after he leaves college. I'm going into business this fall. Have you ever been to California?" Miss Blake admitted that she had never been so far, and Fresno launched himself upon a glowing description of his native State; but before he could shape the conversation to a point where his hearer might perchance express a desire to see its wonders, Still Bill Stover thrust his head cautiously through the door to the bunk-house, and allowed an admiring eye to rove over the transformation.

"Looks like a bazaar!" he exclaimed. "What's the idea?"

"Trainin'-quarters," said Glass.

"Mr. Speed goin' to live here?" inquired the foreman, bringing the remainder of his lanky body into view.

"No, indeed," Jean corrected, "he will merely use this room to train in."

"How do you train in a room?" Stover asked her.

"Why, you—just train, I suppose." Miss Chapin turned to Glass. "How does a person train in a room?"

"Why, he—just trains, that's all. A guy can't train without trainin'-quarters, can he?"

"We thought it would make a nice gymnasium," offered Miss Blake.

"Looks like business." Stover's admiration was keen. "I rode over to Gallagher's place last night and laid our bets."

"How much have you wagered?" asked Fresno.

"More'n we can afford to lose."

"But you aren't going to lose," Miss Blake said, enthusiastically.

"I got Gallagher to play some records for me."

"Silas on Fifth Avenue?"

"Sure! And The Holy City, too! Willie stayed out by the barb-wire fence; he didn't dast to go in. When I come out I found him ready to cry. That desperado has sure got the heart of a woman. I reckon he'd commit a murder for that phonograph—he's so full of sentiment."

Fresno spoke sympathetically.

"It's a fortunate thing for you fellows that Speed came when he did. I'm anxious for him to beat this cook, and I hate to see him so careless with his training."

"Careless!" cried Helen.

"What's he done?" inquired Stover.

"Nothing, so far. That's the trouble. He's sure he can win, but" —Fresno shook his head, doubtfully—"there's such a thing as overconfidence. No matter how good a man may be, he should take care of himself."

"What's wrong with his trainin'?" demanded Glass.

"I think he ought to have more rest. It's too noisy around the house; he can't get enough sleep."

"Nor anybody else," agreed Glass, meaningly; "there's too much singin'."

"That's funny," said Stover. "Music soothes me, no matter how bad it is. Last night when we come back from the Centipede Mr. Fresno was singin' Dearie, but I dozed right off in the middle of it. An' it's the same way with cattle. They like it. It's part of a man's duty when he's night-ridin' a herd to pizen the atmosphere with melody."

"What I mean to say is this," Fresno hastened to explain. "We keep late hours at the house, whereas an athlete ought to retire early and arise with the sun. I thought it would be a good scheme to have Mr. Speed sleep out here until the race is over, where he won't be disturbed. Nine o'clock is bedtime for a man in training."

"Oh, I don't think that is at all necessary," said Miss Blake quickly.

"We can't afford to spoil his chances," argued the young man. "There is too much at stake. Am I right, Mr. Glass?"

Now, like most fat men, Lawrence Glass was fond of his rest, and since his arrival at the Flying Heart his sleeping-hours had been shortened considerably, so for once he agreed with the Californian. "No question about it," said he. "And I'll sleep here with him if you'll put a couple of cots in the place."

"But suppose Mr. Speed won't do it?" questioned Miss Blake.

"You ask him, and he won't refuse," said Jean.

"We don't want to see him defeated," urged Helen's other suitor; at which the girl rose, saying doubtfully:

"Of course I'll do my best, if you think it's really important."

"Thank you," said Stover gratefully, while Fresno congratulated himself upon an easy victory. "I'll ask him at once, but you must come along, Jean, and you too, Mr. Glass."

The two girls took Speed's trainer with them, and went forth in search of the young man.

"It's up to you fellows to see that he gets to bed early," said Fresno, when he and Stover were alone.

"Leave it to us. And as for gettin' up, we turn out at daylight. I don't reckon he could sleep none after that if he tried." Stover pointed to the striped elastic coils of the exerciser against the wall. "I didn't want to speak about it while they was here," said he, "but one of them young ladies lost her garters."

"That's not a pair of garters, that's a chest-weight."

"Jest wait for what?"

"Chest-weight—chest-developer."

"Oh!" Stover examined the device curiously, "I thought a chest-developer came in a bottle."

Fresno explained the operation of the apparatus, at which the cow-man remarked, admiringly: "That young feller is all right, ain't he?"

"Think so?"

"Sure! Don't you?"

Fresno explained his doubts by a crafty lift of his brows and a shrug. "I thought so—at first."

Stover wheeled upon him abruptly. "What's wrong?"

"Oh, nothing."

After a pause the foreman remarked, vaguely, "He's the intercollegit champeen of Yale."

"Oh no, hardly that, or I would have heard of him."

"Ain't he no champeen?"

"Champion of the running broad smile and the half-mile talk perhaps."

"Ain't he a foot-runner?"

"Perhaps. I've never seen him run, but I have my doubts."

"Good Lord!" moaned Stover, weakly.

"He may be the best sprinter in the country, mind you, but I'll lay a little bet that he can't run a hundred yards without sustenance."

"Without what?"

"Sustenance—something to eat."

"Well, we've got plenty for him to eat," said the mystified foreman.

"You don't understand. However, time will tell."

"But we ain't got no time. We've made this race 'pay or play,' a week from Saturday, and the bets are down. We was afraid the Centipede would welsh when they seen who we had, so we framed it that-away. What's to be done?"

Again Fresno displayed an artistic restraint that was admirable. "It's none of my business," said he, with a careless shrug.

"I—I guess I'll tell Willie and the boys," vouchsafed Bill apprehensively.

"No! no! Don't breathe a word I've said to you. He may be a crackerjack, and I wouldn't do him an injustice for the world. All the same, I wish he hadn't broken my stop-watch."

"D'you think he broke it a-purpose?"

"What do you think?"

Stover mopped the sweat from his brow.

"Can't we time him with a ordinary watch?"

"Sure. We can take yours. It won't be exact, but—"

"I ain't got no watch. I bet mine last night at the Centipede. Willie's got one, though."

"Mind you, he may be all right," Fresno repeated, reassuringly; then hearing the object of their discussion approaching with his trainer, the two strolled out through the bunk-room, Stover a prey to a new-born suspicion, Fresno musing to himself that diplomacy was not a lost art.

"You're a fine friend, you are!" Speed exploded, when he and Glass were inside the gymnasium. "What made you say 'yes'?"

"I had to."

"Rot, Larry! You played into Fresno's hands deliberately! Now I've got to spend my evenings in bed while he sits in the hammock and sings Dearie." He shook his head gloomily. "Who knows what may happen?"

"It will do you good to get some sleep, Wally."

"But I don't want to sleep!" cried the exasperated suitor. "I want to make love. Do you think I came all the way from New York to sleep? I can do that at Yale."

"Take it from me, Bo, you've got plenty of time to win that dame. Eight hours is a workin' day anywhere."

"My dear fellow, the union hours for courting don't begin until 9 P.M. I've got myself into a fine mess, haven't I? Just when Night spreads her sable mantle and Dan Cupid strings up his bow, I must forsake my lady-love and crawl into the hay. Oh, you're a good trainer!"

"You'd better can some of this love-talk and think more about foot-racin'."

"It can't be done! Nine o'clock! The middle of the afternoon. It's rather funny, though, isn't it?" Speed was not the sort to cherish even a real grievance for any considerable time. "If it had happened to anybody else I'd laugh myself sick."

Glass chuckled. "The whole thing is a hit. Look at this joint, for instance." He took in their surroundings with a comprehensive gesture. "It looks about as much like a gymnasium as I look like a contortionist. Why don't you get a Morris chair and a mandolin?"

"There are two reasons," said Speed, facetiously. "First, it takes an athlete to get out of a Morris chair; and, second, a mandolin has proved to be many a young man's ruin."

Glass examined the bow of ribbon upon the lonesome piece of exercising apparatus.

"It looks like the trainin'-stable for the Colonial Dames. What a yelp this place would be to Covington or any other athlete."

"It is not an athletic gymnasium." Speed smiled as he lighted a cigarette. "It is a romantic gymnasium. As Socrates once observed—"

"Socrates! I'm hep to him," Glass interrupted, quickly. "I trained a Greek professor once and got wised up on all that stuff. Socrates was the—the Hemlock Kid."

"Exactly! As Socrates, the Hemlock Kid, deftly put it, 'In hoc signature vintage.'"

"I don't get you."

"That is archaic Scandinavian, and, translated, means, 'Love cannot thrive without her bower.'"

"No answer to that telegram yet, eh?"

"Hardly time."

"Better wire Covington again, hadn't you? Mebbe he didn't get it?"

"I promised Mrs. Keap that I would, but—" Speed lost himself abruptly in speculation, for he did not know exactly how to manage this unexpected complication. Of one thing only was he certain: it would require some thought.

"Say, Wally, suppose Covington don't come?"

"Then I shall sprain my ankle," said the other. "Hello! What in the world—" Still Bill Stover and Willie came into the room carrying an armful of lumber. Behind them followed Carara with a huge wooden tub, and Cloudy rolling a kerosene barrel.

"Where do you want it, gents?" inquired the foreman.

"Where do we want what?"

"The shower-bath."

"Shower—I didn't order a shower-bath!"

"No; but we aim to make it as pleasant for you as we can."

"If there is anything I abhor, it's a shower-bath!" exclaimed the athlete.

"You just got to have one. Mr. Fresno said all this gymnasium lacked was a shower-bath, a pair of scales, and a bulletin-board. He said you'd sure need a bath after workin' that chest-developer. We ain't got no scales, nor no board, but we'll toggle up some sort of a bath for you. The blacksmith's makin' a squirter to go on the bar'l."

"Very well, put it wherever you wish. I sha'n't use it."

"I wouldn't overlook nothin', if I was you," said Willie, in even milder tones than Stover had used.

"You overwhelm me with these little attentions," retorted Mr. Speed.

"Where you goin' to run to-day?" inquired the first speaker.

"I don't know. Why?"

"We thought you might do a hundred yards agin time."

"Nix!" interposed Glass, hurriedly. "I can't let him overdo at the start. Besides, we ain't got no stop-watch."

"I got a reg'lar watch," said Willie, "and I can catch you pretty close. We'd admire to see you travel some, Mr. Speed."

But Glass vowed that he was in charge of his protege's health, and would not permit it. Once outside, however, he exclaimed: "That's more of Fresno's work, Wally! I tell you, he's Jerry. He'll rib them pirates to clock you, and if they do—well, you'd better keep runnin', that's all."

"You can do me a favor," said Speed. "Buy that watch."

"There's other watches on the farm."

"Buy them all, and bring me the bill."

Before setting out on his daily grind, Speed announced to his trainer that he had decided to take him along for company, and when that corpulent gentleman rebelled on the ground that the day was too sultry, his employer would have none of it, so together they trotted away later in the morning, Speed in his silken suit, Glass running flat-footed and with great effort. But once safely hidden from view, they dropped into a walk, and selecting a favorable resting-place, paused. Speed lighted a cigarette, Glass produced a deck of cards from his pocket, and they played seven- up. Having covered five miles in this exhausting fashion, they returned to the ranch in time for luncheon. Both ate heartily, for the exercise had agreed with them.

CHAPTER VIII

Lawrence Glass was beginning to like New Mexico. Not only did it afford a tinge of romance, discernable in the deep, haunting eyes of Mariedetta, the maid, but it offered an opportunity for financial advancement—as, for instance, the purchase of Willie's watch. This timepiece cost the trainer twenty-one dollars, and he sold it to Speed for double the amount, believing in the luck of even numbers. Nor did young Speed allow his trainer's efforts to cease here, for in every portable timepiece on the ranch he recognized a menace, and not until Lawrence had cornered the market and the whole collection was safely locked in his trunk did he breathe easily. This required two days, during which the young people at the ranch enjoyed themselves thoroughly. They were halcyon days for the Yale man, for Fresno was universally agreeable, and seemed resigned to the fact that Helen should prefer his rival's company to his own. Even when Speed had regretfully dragged himself off to bed in the evening, the plump tenor amused Miss Blake by sounding the suitor's praises as an athlete, reports of which pleased Wally intensely. Mr. Fresno was a patient person, who realized fully the fact that a fall is not painful unless sustained from a considerable height.

As for Glass, he recounted tales of Mariedetta's capitulation to his employer, and wheezed merrily over the discomfiture of the Mexican girl's former admirers.

"She's a swell little dame," he confided to Speed one afternoon, as they lounged luxuriously in the shade at their customary resting-place. "Yes, and I'm aces with her, too." They had set out for their daily run, and were now contesting for the seven-up supremacy of the Catskill Mountains. Already Glass had been declared the undisputed champion of the Atlantic Coast, while Speed on the day previous had wrested from him the championship of the Mississippi Valley.

"But Mariedetta is dark!" said the college man, as he cut the cards. "She is almost a mulatto."

"Naw! She's no dinge. She's an Aztec, an' them Aztec's is swell people. Say, she can play a guitar like a barber!"

"Miss Blake told me she was in love with Carara."

Glass grunted contemptuously. "I've got it on that insurrects four ways. Why, I'm learning to talk Spanish myself. If he gets flossy, I'll cross one over his bow." The trainer made a vicious jab at an imaginary Mexican. "He ain't got a good wallop in him."

Like all New Yorkers, no matter what their station, Lawrence cherished a provincial contempt for such people as are not of Manhattan. While he was woefully timid in the presence of firearms, and the flash of steel reduced him to a panic, he was a past master at the "manly art," and carried a punch in which he reposed unlimited faith. The deference with which the cowboys treated him, their simple, child-like faith in his every utterance, combined to exaggerate his contempt for them. Even Carara, disappointed in love, treated him with a smiling, backward sort of courtesy which the trainer misconstructed as timidity.

"I thought cowboys was tough guys," continued he, "but it's a mistake. That little Willie, for instance, is a lamb. He packs that Mauser for protection. He's afraid some farmer will walk up and poke his eye out with a corn-cob. One copper with a night-stick could stampede the whole outfit. But they're all right, at that," he acknowledged, magnanimously. "They're a nice bunch of fellers when you know how to take 'em."

"The flies are awful to-day," Speed complained. "They bite my legs."

"I'll bring out a bath robe to-morrow, and we'll hide it in the bushes. I wish there was some place to keep this beer cool." Glass shifted some bottles to a point where the sunlight did not strike them. "I'm getting tired of training, Larry," acknowledged the younger man, with a yawn. "It takes so much time."

Glass shook his head in sympathy. "Seems like we'd ought to hear from Covington," said he.

"He's on his way, no doubt. Isn't it time to go back to the ranch?"

Glass consulted his watch. "No, we ain't done but three miles. Here goes for the rubber."

It was Berkeley Fresno who retreated cautiously from the shelter of a thicket a hundred yards up the arroyo and started briskly homeward, congratulating himself upon the impulse that had decided him to follow the training partners upon their daily routine. He made directly for the corral.

"Which I don't consider there's no consideration comin' to him whatever," said Willie that evening. "He ain't acted on the level."

"Now, see here," objected Stover, "he may be just what he claims he is. Simply because he don't go skally-hootin' around in the hot sun ain't no sign he can't run."

"What about them empty beer bottles?" demanded Willie. "No feller can train on that stuff. I went out there myself and seen 'em. There was a dozen."

"Mebbe Glass drank it. What I claim is this: we ain't got no proof. Fresno is stuck on Miss Blake, and he's a knocker."

"Then let's git some proof, and dam' quick."

"Si, Senores," agreed Carara, who had been an interested listener.

"I agree with you, but we got to be careful—"

Willie grunted with disgust.

"—we can't go at it like we was killin' snakes. Mr. Speed is a guest here."

Again the little gun man expressed his opinion, this time in violet-tinted profanity, and the other cowboys joined in.

"All the same he is a guest, and no rough work goes. I'm in charge while Mr. Chapin is away, and I'm responsible."

"Senor Bill," Carara ventured, "the fat vaquero, he is no guest. He is one of us."

"That's right," seconded Willie. "He's told us all along that Mr. Speed was a Merc'ry-footed wonder, and if the young feller can't run he had ought to have told us."

Mr. Cloudy showed his understanding of the discussion by nodding silently.

"We'll put it up to him in the morning," said Stover.

"If Mr. Speed cannot r-r-run, w'at you do, eh?" questioned the Mexican.

Nobody answered. Still Bill seemed at a loss for words, Mr. Cloudy stared gloomily into space, and Willie ground his teeth.

On the following morning Speed sought a secluded nook with Helen, but no sooner had he launched himself fairly upon the subject uppermost in his mind than he was disturbed by a delegation of cowboys, consisting of the original four who had waited upon him that first morning after his arrival. They came forward with grave and serious mein, requesting a moment's interview. It was plain there was something of more than ordinary importance upon their minds from the manner in which Stover spoke, but when Helen quickly volunteered to withdraw, Speed checked her.

"Stay where you are; I have no secrets from you," said he. Then noting the troubled face of the foreman, quoted impatiently:

"'You may fire when ready, Gridley.'"

Still Bill shifted the lump in his cheek, and cleared his throat before beginning formally.

"Mr. Speed, while we honor you a heap for your accomplishments, and while we believe in you as a man and a champeen, we kind of feel that it might make you stretch your legs some if you knew just exactly what this foot-race means to the Flying Heart outfit."

"I assured you that the Centipede cook would be beaten," said the college man, stiffly.

"Isn't Mr. Speed's word sufficient?" inquired the girl.

Stover bowed. "It had sure ought to be, and we thank you for them new assurances. You see, our spiritual on-rest is due to the fact that Humpy Joe's get-away left us broke, and we banked on you to pull us even. That first experience strained our credulity to the bustin' point, and—well, in words of one syllable, we come from Joplin."

"Missouri," said Willie.

"My dear sirs, I can't prove that you are going to win your wagers until the day of the race. However, if you are broke to start with, I don't see how you can expect to lose a great deal."

"You ain't got the right angle on the affair," Stover explained. "Outside of the onbearable contumely of losin' twice to this Centipede outfit, which would be bad enough, we have drawn a month's wages in advance, and we have put it up. Moreover, I have bet my watch, which was presented to me by the officials of the Santa Fe for killin' a pair of road-agents when I was Depity Sheriff."

Miss Blake uttered a little scream, and Speed regarded the lanky speaker with new interest. "It's a Waltham movement, solid gold case, eighteen jewels, and engraved with my name."

"No wonder you prize it," said Wally.

"I bet my saddle," informed Carara, in his slow, soft dialect. "Stamp' leather wit' silver filagree. It is more dear to me than — well—I love it ver' much, Senor!"

"Seems like Willie has made the extreme sacrifice," Stover followed up. "While all our boys has gone the limit, Willie has topped 'em all: he's bet his gun."

"Indeed! Is it a good weapon?"

"It's been good to me," said the little man, dryly. "I took it off the quivering remains of a Sheriff in Dodge City, up to that time the best hip shot in Kansas."

Speed felt a cold chill steal up his spine, while Miss Blake went pale and laid a trembling hand upon his arm.

"You see it ain't intrinsic value so much as association and sentiment that leads to this interview," Stover continued. "It ain't no joke—we don't joke with the Centipede—and we've relied on you. The Mex here would do murder for that saddle," Carara nodded, and breathed something in his own tongue. "I have parted with my honor, and Willie is gamblin' just as high."

"But I notice Mr.—Willie still has his revolver."

"Sure I got it!" Willie laughed, abruptly. "And I don't give it up till we lose, neither. That's the understandin'." His voice was surprisingly harsh for one so high-pitched. He looked more like a professor than ever.

"Willie has reasons for his caution which we respect," explained the spokesman.

J. Wallingford Speed, face to face with these serious-minded gentlemen, began to reflect that this foot-race was not a thing to be taken too lightly.

"I can't understand," he declared, with a touch of irritation, "why you should risk such priceless things upon a friendly encounter."

"Friendly!" cried Willie and Stover in a tone that made their listeners gasp. "The Centipede and the Flying Heart is just as friendly as a pair of wild boars."

"You see, it's a good thing we wised you up," added the latter.

Carara muttered fiercely: "Senor, I works five year' for that saddle. I am a good gambler, si, si! but I keel somebody biffore I lose it to the Centipede."

"And is that Echo Phonograph worth all this?" inquired Helen.

"We won that phonograph at risk of life and limb," said Willie, doggedly, "from the Centipede-"

"—and twenty other outfits, Senor."

"It's a trophy," declared the foreman, "and so long as it ain't where it belongs, the Flying Heart is in disgrace."

"Even the 'Leven X treats us scornful!" cried the smallest of the trio angrily. "We're a joke to the whole State."

"I know just how these gentlemen must feel," declared Miss Blake, tactfully, at which Stover bowed with grateful awkwardness.

"And it's really a wonderful instrument," said he. "I don't reckon there's another one like it in the world, leastways in these parts. You'd ought to hear it—clear as a bell—"

"And sweet," said Willie. "God! It's sure sweet!"

"Why, we was a passel of savages on this ranch till we got it—no sentiment, no music, no nothin' in our souls—except profanity and thirst. Then everything changed." Stover nodded gravely. "We got gentle. That music mellered us up. We got so we was as full of brotherly love as a basket of kittens. Some of the boys commenced writin' home; Cloudy begin to pay his poker debts. You'd scarcely hear enough profanity to make things bearable. I tell you it was refined. It got so that when a man came steamin' in after a week's high life and low company in town, his wages gone, and his stummick burnin' like he'd swallered all his cigar- butts, it didn't make no difference if he found a herd of purple crocodiles in his blankets, or the bunk-house walls a-crawlin' with Gila monsters. Little things like that wouldn't phaze him! He'd switch on the Echo Phonograph and doze off like a babe in arms, for the tender notes of Madam-o-sella Melby in The Holy City would soothe and comfort him like the caressin' hand of a young female woman."

"I begin to feel your loss," said Speed, gravely. "Gentlemen, I can only assure you I shall do my best."

"Then you won't take no chances?" inquired Willie, mildly.

"You may rely upon me to take care of myself."

"Thank you!" The delegation moved away.

"What d'you think of him?" inquired Stover of the little man in glasses, when they were out of hearing.

"I think he's all right," Willie hesitated, "only kind of crazy, like all Eastern boys. It don't seem credible that no sane man would dast to bluff after what we've said. He'd be flyin' in the face of Providence."

But this comforting conclusion wavered again, when Berkeley Fresno, who had awaited their report, scoffed openly.

"He can't run! If he could run he'd be running. I tell you, he can't run as fast as a sheep can walk."

"Senor, you see those beautiful medal he have?" expostulated Carara.

"Sure," agreed Willie. "His brisket was covered with 'em. He had one that hung down like a dewlap."

"Phony!"

"I've killed men for less," muttered the stoop-shouldered man.

"Did you see his legs?" Fresno was bent upon convincing his hearers.

"Couldn't help but see 'em in that runnin'-suit."

"Nice and soft and white, weren't they?"

"They didn't look like dark meat," Stover agreed, reluctantly. "But you can't go nothin' on the looks of a feller's legs."

"Well, then, take his wind. A runner always has good lungs, but I'll bet if you snapped him on the chest with a rubber band he'd cough himself to death."

"Mebbe he ain't in good shape yet."

Fresno sneered. "No, and he'll never get into good condition with those girls hanging around him all the time. Don't you know that the worst thing in the world for an athlete is to talk to a woman?"

"That's the worst thing in the world for anybody," said Willie, with cynicism. "But how can we stop it?"

"Make him eat as well as sleep in his training-quarters; don't let him spend any time whatever in female company. Keep your eyes on him night and day."

Willie spoke his mind deliberately. "I'm in favor of that. If this is another Humpy Joe affair I'm a-goin' to put one more notch in my gun-handle, and it looks like a cub bear had chawed it already."

"There ain't but one thing to do," Stover announced, firmly. "We've got to put it up to Mr. Glass and learn the truth."

"You'll find him in the bunk-house," directed Fresno. "I think I'll trail along and hear what he has to say."

CHAPTER IX

Glass had gone to the cowboys' sleeping-quarters in search of his employer, and was upon the point of leaving when the delegation filed in. He regarded them with careless contempt, and removed his clay pipe to exclaim, cheerfully:

"B—zoo gents! Where's my protege?"

"I don't know. Where did you have it last?"

"I mean Speed, my trainin' partner. That's a French word."

"Oh! We just left him."

"Think I'll hunt him up."

"Wait a minute." Willie came forward. "Let's talk."

"All right. We'll visit. Let her go, professor."

"You've been handlin' him for quite a spell, haven't you?"

"Sure! It's my trainin' that put him where he is. Ask him if it ain't."

"Then he's a good athlete, is he?"

"Is he good? Huh!" Glass grunted, expressively.

"How fast can he do a hundred yards?"

Larry yawned as if this conversation bored him.

"Oh—about—eight—seconds."

At this amazing declaration Willie paused, as if to thoroughly digest it.

"Eight seconds!" repeated the little man at length.

"Sure! Depends on how he feels, of course."

Berkeley Fresno, in the corner, snickered audibly, at which the trainer scowled at him.

"Think he can't do it, eh? Well, he's there four ways from the ace."

Seeing no evidence that his statement failed to carry conviction in other quarters at least, Glass went further. It was so easy to string these simple-minded people that he could not resist the temptation. "Didn't you never hear about the killin' he made at Saratoga?" he queried.

Willie started, and his hand crept slowly backward along his belt. "Killin'! Is that his game?"

"Now, get me right," explained the former speaker. "He breaks trainin', and goes up to Saratoga for a little rest. While he's there he wins eight thousand dollars playin' diabolo."

"Playin' what?" queried Stover.

"Diabolo! He backs himself, of course."

Glass took an imaginary spool from his pocket, spun it by means of an imaginary string, then sent it aloft and pretended to catch it dexterously. The cowboys watched him with grave, uncomprehending eyes.

"He starts with a case five and runs it up to eight thousand dollars, that's all."

Stover uttered an exclamation of astonishment, whereupon the New-Yorker grew even bolder.

"The next week he hops over to Bar Harbor and wins the Furturity Ping-pong stakes from scratch. That's worth twenty thousand if it's worth a lead nickel. Oh, I guess he's there, all right!" He searched out a match and relighted his pipe.

"I suppose he's a great croquet-player too," observed Fresno, whose face was purple.

"Sure!" Glass winked at him, glad to see that the Californian enjoyed this kind of sport.

"We don't care nothin' about his skill at sleight-of-hand tricks," said the man in spectacles, seriously. "And we wouldn't hold his croquet habits agin him. Some men drink, some gamble, some do worse; every man has his weakness, and croquet may be his. What we want to know is this: can he win our phonograph?"

"Surest thing you know!"

"Then you vouch for him, do you?" Willie's eyes were bent upon the fat man with a look of searching gravity that warned Glass not to temporize.

"With my life!" exclaimed the trainer.

"You're on!" said the cowboy, with unexpected grimness.

"What d'you mean?"

But before the other could explain, Berkeley Fresno, who had sunk weakly into a chair at Larry's extravagant praise of his rival, afforded a diversion. The tenor had leaned back, convulsed with enjoyment when, losing his balance, he came to the floor with a crash. The sudden sound brought a terrifying result, for with a startled cry the undersized cow-man leaped as if touched by a living flame. Like a flash of light he whirled and poised on his toes, his long, evil-looking revolver drawn and cocked, his tense face vulturelike and fierce. His eyes glared through his spectacles, his livid features worked as if at the sound of his own death-call. His whole frame was tense; a galvanic current had transformed him. His weapon darted toward the spot whence the noise had come, and he would have fired blindly had not Stover yelled:

"Don't shoot!"

Willie paused, and the breath crept audibly into his lungs.

"Who done that?" he asked, harshly.

Still Bill brought his lanky frame up above the level of the table.

"God 'lmighty! don't be so sudden, Willie!" he cried. "It was a accident."

But the gun man seemed unconvinced. With cat-like tread he stole cautiously to the door, and stared out into the sunlight; then, seeing nobody in sight, he replaced his weapon in its resting-place and sighed with relief.

"I thought it was the marshal from Waco," he said. "He'll never git me alive."

Stover addressed himself to Fresno, who had gone pale, and was still prostrate where he had fallen.

"Get up, Mr. Berkeley, but don't make no more moves like that behind a man's back. He most got you."

Fresno arose in a daze and mopped his brow, murmuring, weakly, "I-I didn't mean to."

Carara and Mr. Cloudy came out from cover whither they had fled at Willie's first movement. "I dreamed about that feller agin last night," apologized the little man. "I'm sort of nervous, and any sudden noise sets me off."

As for Glass, that corpulent individual had disappeared as if into thin air; only a stir in one of the bunks betrayed his hiding-place. At the first sight of Willie's revolver he had dived for a refuge and was now flattened against the wall, a pillow pressed over his head to deaden the expected report.

"Hey!" called the foreman, but Glass did not hear him.

"Seems to be gun-shy," observed Willie, gently.

Stover crossed to the bunk and laid a hand upon the occupant, at which a convulsion ran through the trainer's soft body, and it became as rigid as if locked in death. "Come out, Mr. Glass, it's all over."

Larry muttered in a stifled voice, "Go 'way!"

"It was a mistake."

He opened his tight-shut lids, rolled over, and thrust forth a round, pallid face. He saw Stover laughing, and beheld the white teeth of Carara, the Mexican, who said:

"Perhaps the Senor is sleepy!"

Finding himself the object of what seemed to him a particularly senseless joke, the New-Yorker crept forth, his face suffused with anger. Strangely enough, he still retained the pipe in his fingers.

"Say, are youse guys tryin' to kid me?" he demanded, roughly. Now that no firearm was in sight, he was master of himself again; and seeing the cause of his undignified alarm leaning against the table, he stepped toward him threateningly. "If you try that again, young feller, I'll chip you on the jaw, and give you a long, dreamy nap." He thrust a short, square fist under Willie's nose.

That scholarly gentleman straightened up, and edged his way to one side, Glass following aggressively.

"You're a husky, ain't you?" said the little man, squinting up at the red face above him. "Am I?" Glass snorted. "Take a good look!"

With deliberate menace he bumped violently into the other. It was with difficulty he could restrain himself from crushing him.

Stover gasped and retreated, while Carara crossed himself, then sidled back of a bunk. Mr. Cloudy stepped silently out through the open door and held his thumbs.

"You start to kid me and I'll wallop you—"

"One moment!" Willie was transfigured suddenly. An instant since he had been a stoop-shouldered, short-sighted, insignificant person, more gentle mannered than a child, but in a flash he became a palpitating fury: an evil atom surcharged with such terrific venom that his antagonist drew back involuntarily. "Don't you make no threat'nin' moves in my direction, or you'll go East in an ice-bath!" He was panting as if the effort to hold himself in leash was almost more than he could stand.

"G'wan!" said Glass, thickly.

"You're deluded with the idea that the Constitution made all men equal, but it didn't; it was Mr. Colt." With a movement quicker than light the speaker drew his gun for the second time, and buried half the barrel in the New-Yorker's ribs.

"Look out!" Glass barked the words, and undertook to deflect the weapon with his hand.

"Let it alone or it'll go off!"

Glass dropped his hand as if it had been burned, and stared down his bulging front with horrified, fascinated eyes.

"Now, listen. We've stood for you as long as we can. You've made your talk and got away with it, but from now on you're working for us. We've framed a foot-race, and put up our panga because you said you had a champeen. Now, we ain't sayin' you lied—'cause if we thought you had, I'd gut-shoot you here, now." Willie paused, while Glass licked his lips and undertook to frame a reply. The black muzzle of the weapon hovering near his heart, however, stupefied him. Mechanically he thrust the stem of his pipe between his lips while Willie continued to glare at him balefully. "You're boss is a guest, but you ain't. We can talk plain to you."

"Y—yes, of course."

"You said just now you'd answer for him with your life. Well, we aim to make you! We ain't a-goin' to lose this foot-race under no circumstances whatever, so we give you complete authority over the body, health, and speed of Mr. Speed. It's up to you to make him beat that cook."

"S-s-suppose he gets sick or sprains his ankle?" Glass undertook to move his body from in front of the weapon, but it followed him as if magnetized.

"There ain't a-goin' to be no accidents or excuses. It's pay or play, money at the tape. You're his trainer, and it's your fault if he ain't fit when he toes the mark. Understand?"

Willie lowered the muzzle of his weapon, and fired between the legs of Glass, who leaped into the air with all the grace of a gazelle. It was due to no conscious action on his part that the trainer leaped; his muscles were stimulated spasmodically, and propelled him from the floor. At the same time his will was so utterly paralyzed that he had no control over his movements; he did not even hear the yell that burst from his throat as his lungs contracted; he merely knew that he was in the supremest peril, and that flight was futile. Therefore he undertook to steady himself. Every tissue of his body seemed to creep and crawl. The flesh inside his legs was quivering, the close-cropped hair of his thick neck rose and prickled, and his capacious abdomen throbbed and pulsated like a huge bowl of jelly. He laid his hands upon it to still the disturbance. Then he became conscious that he had bitten his pipe-stem in two and swallowed the end. He felt it sticking in his throat.

"Did you hear what I said?" demanded Willie, in a voice that sounded like the sawing of a meat bone.

Glass opened his mouth, and when no sound issued, nodded.

"And you understand?"

Again the trainer bobbed his head. The pipe-stem had cut off all power of speech, and he knew himself dumb for life.

"Then I guess that's all. It's up to you." Willie replaced his gun, and the fat man threatened to fall. "Come on, boys!" The cowboys filed out silently, but on the threshold Willie paused and darted a venomous glance at his enemy. "Don't forget what I said about Mr. Colt and the equality of man."

"Yes, sir!—yes, ma'am!" ejaculated the frightened trainer, nervously. When they were gone he collapsed.

"They are rather severe, aren't they?" ventured Fresno.

"Severe!" cried the unhappy man. "Why, Speed can't—" He was about to explain everything when the memory of Willie's words smote him like a blow. That fiend had threatened to kill him, Lawrence Glass, without preliminary if it became evident that a fraud had been practiced. Manifestly this was no place for hysterical confidences. Larry's mouth closed like a trap, while the Californian watched him intently. At length he did speak, but in a strangely softened tone, and at utter variance with his custom.

"Say, Mr. Fresno! Which direction is New York?"

"That way." Fresno pointed to the east, and the other man stared longingly out through the bunk-house window.

"It's quite a walk, ain't it?"

"Walk?" Berkeley laughed. "It's two or three thousand miles!" Glass sighed heavily. "Why do you ask?"

"Oh, nothin'. Jest gettin' homesick." He calmed himself with an effort, entered the gymnasium as if in search of something, and then set forth to find Speed.

That ecstatic young gentleman wrenched his gaze away from the blue eyes of Miss Blake to see his trainer signalling him from afar.

"What is it, Lawrence?"

"Got to see you."

"Presently."

"Nix! I got to see you now!" Glass's ruddy face was blotched, and he seemed to rest in the grip of some blighting malady. Beneath his arm he carried a tight-rolled bundle. Sensing something important back of this unusual demeanor, Speed excused himself and followed Larry, who did not trust to speech until they were alone in the gymnasium with the doors closed. Then he unrolled the bundle he carried, spread it upon the floor, and stepped into its exact centre.

"Are you standing on my prayer-rug?" demanded his companion, angrily.

"I am! And from this on I'm goin' to make it work itself to death. She said a feller couldn't get hurt if he stood on it and said 'Allah.' Well, I'm goin' to wear it out."

"What's wrong?"

"Do you know what's goin' to happen to me if Covington don't get here and beat this cook?"

"Happen to you?"

"Yes, me! These outlaws have put it up to me to win this bet for them."

"Well, Covington can beat anybody."

"But Covington isn't here yet."

"Not yet, but—" The young man smiled. "You're not frightened, are you?"

"Scared to death, that's all," acknowledged the other. Then when his employer laughed openly, he broke out at a white-heat. "Joke, eh? Well, you'd better have a good laugh while you can, because Humpy Joe's finish will be a ten-course dinner to what you'll get if Covington misses his train."

"How easily frightened you are!"

"Yes? Well, any time people start shooting shots I'm too big for this earth. The hole in a gun looks as big as a gas-tank to me."

"But nobody is going to shoot you!" exclaimed the mystified college man.

"They ain't, hey? I missed the Golden Stairs by a lip not half an hour ago. I got a pipe-stem crossways in my gullet now, and it tickles." He coughed loudly, then shook his head. "No use; it won't come up." With feverish intensity he told of his narrow escape from destruction, the memory bringing a sweat of agony to his brow. "And the worst of it is," he concluded, "I'm 'marked' with guns. I've always been that way."

"Tut! tut! Don't alarm yourself. If Covington shouldn't come, the race will be declared off."

"No chance," announced the trainer, with utter conviction. "These thugs have made it pay or play, and the bets are down."

"You know I can't run."

"If he don't come, you'll have to!"

"Absurd! I shall be indisposed."

"If you mean you'll get sick, or sprain an ankle, or break a leg, or kill yourself, guess again. I'm responsible for you now. Something may go wrong with me, that pipe-stem is liable to gimme a cancer, but nothin' is goin' to happen to you. My only chance to make a live of it is to cough up that clay, and get some one to outrun this cook. You're the only chance I've got, if Culver don't show, and the first law of nature ain't never been repealed."

"Self-protection, eh?"

"Exactly." Glass coughed thrice without result, stepped off the prayerrug, rolled it up tightly; then, hugging it beneath his arm, went on: "That four-eyed guy slipped me a whole lot of feed-box information. Why, he's a killer, Wally! And he's got a cash-register to tally his dead."

"Notches on his gun-handle, I suppose?"

"So many that it looks like his wife had used it to hang pictures with. I tell you, he's the most deceitful rummy I ever seen. What's more, he's got the homicide habit, and the habit has got its eye on me." Glass was in deadly earnest, and his alarm contrasted so strongly with his former contemptuous attitude toward the cowboys that Speed was constrained to laugh again.

"It's the most amusing thing I ever heard of."

"Yes," said the trainer, with elaborate sarcasm, "it would be awful funny if it wasn't on the square." He moistened his lip nervously.

"You alarm yourself unnecessarily. We'll hear from Culver soon, either by wire or in person. He's never failed me yet. But if I were you, Larry, I'd leave that Mexican girl alone."

"Mary?"

"Yes. Mariedetta. Now, there's something to be afraid of. If these cowboys are in love with her and have their eyes on you—"

"Oh, Willie ain't her steady, and he's the only one I'm leary of. Mary's beau is that Egyptian with the funny clothes, and I can lick any guy with tight pants."

A gentle knock sounded at the door, at which Speed called:

"Come in!"

Senor Aurelio Maria Carara entered. He was smoking his customary corn-husk cigarette, but his dark eyes were grave and his silken mustachios were pointed to the fineness of a bristle.

CHAPTER X

"Buenos dias, Senor." Carara bowed politely to Speed.

"Good-morning again," said Wally.

Turning to the trainer, Carara eyed him from top to toe, removed his cigarette, and flipped the ashes daintily from it; then, smiling disdainfully, said:

"Buenos dias, Senor Fat!"

Glass started. "You talkin' to me?"

"Yes." Carara leaned languidly against the wall, took a match from his pocket, and dextrously struck it between the nails of his thumb and finger. He breathed his lungs full of smoke and exhaled it through his nose. "I would have spik to you biffore, but the Senor Fat is"—he shrugged his shoulders—"frighten' so bad he will not understan'. So—I come back."

"Who's scared?" said Glass, gruffly.

Carara turned his palm outward, in gentle apology.

"You been talk' a gret deal to my Senorita—to Mariedetta, eh?"

"Oh, the Cuban Queen!" Glass winked openly at Speed. "Sure! I slip her a laugh now and then."

"She is not Cubana, she is Mexicana," said Carara, politely.

"Well, what d'you think of that! I thought she was a Cuban." Glass began to chuckle.

"Senor Fat," broke in the Mexican, sharply, while Larry winced at the distasteful appellation, "she is my Senorita!"

"Is she? Well, I can't help it if she falls for me." The speaker cast an appreciative glance at his employer. "And you can cut out that 'Senor Fat,' because it don't go—" Then he gasped, for Carara slowly drew from inside his shirt a long, thin-bladed knife bearing marks of recent grinding, and his black eyes snapped. His face had become suddenly convulsed, while his voice rang with the tone of chilled metal. Glass retreated a step, a shudder ran through him, and his eyes riveted themselves upon the weapon with horrified intensity.

"Listen, Pig! If you spik to her again, I will cut you." The gaze of the Mexican pierced his victim. "I will not keel you, I will just—cut you!"

Speed, who had sat in open-mouthed amazement during the scene, pinched himself. Like Larry, he could not remove his gaze from the swarthy man. He pulled himself together with an effort, however, undertaking to divert the present trend of the conversation.

"W—where will you cut him?" he asked, pleasantly, more to make conversation than from any lingering question as to the precise location.

"Here." Carara turned the blade against himself, and traced a cross upon his front, whereupon the trainer gurgled and laid protecting hands upon his protruding abdomen. "You spik Spanish?"

"No." Glass shook his head.

"But you understan' w'at I try to say?"

"Yes—oh yes—I'm hep all right."

"And the Senor Fat will r-r-re-member?"

"Sure!" Glass sighed miserably, and tearing his eyes away from the glittering blade, rolled them toward his employer. "I don't want her! Mr. Speed knows I don't want her!"

Carara bowed. "And the Fat Senor will not spik wit' her again?"

"No!"

"Gracias, Senor! I thank you!"

"You're welcome!" agreed the New Yorker, with repressed feeling.

"Adios! Adios, Senor Speed!"

"Good-bye!" exclaimed the two in chorus.

Carara returned the knife to its hiding-place, swept the floor gracefully with his sombrero, then placing the spangled head-piece at an exact angle upon his raven locks, lounged out, his silver spurs tinkling in the silence.

Glass took a deep breath.

"He doesn't mean to kill you—just cut you," said Speed. "I got it," declared the other, fervently. Again he laid repressing hands upon his bulging front and looked down at it tenderly. "They've all got it in for my pad, haven't they?"

"I told you to keep away from that girl."

"Humph!" Glass spoke with soulful conviction. "Take it from me, Bo, I'll walk around her as if she was a lake. Who'd ever think that chorus-man was a killer?"

"Surely you don't care for her seriously?"

"Not now. I—I love my Cuban, but"—he quivered apprehensively—"I'll bet that rummy packs a 'shiv' in every pocket."

From outside the bunk-house came the low, musical notes of a quail, and Glass puckered his lips to answer, then grew pale. "That's her," he declared, in a panic. "I've got a date with her."

"Are you going to keep it?"

"Not for a nose-bag full of gold nuggets! Take a look, Wally, and see what she's doing."

Speed did as directed. "She's waiting."

"Let her wait," breathed the trainer.

"Here comes Stover and Willie."

"More bad news." Glass unrolled his prayer-rug, and stepped upon it hastily. "Say, what's that word? Quick! You know! The password. Quick!"

"Allah!"

"That's her!" The fat man began to mumble thickly. It was plain that his spirit was utterly broken.

But this call was prompted purely by solicitude, it seemed. Willie had little to say, and Stover, ignoring all mention of the earlier encounter he had witnessed, exclaimed:

"There's been some queer goin's-on 'round here, Mr. Speed. Have you noticed 'em?"

"No. What sort?"

"Well, the other mornin' I discovered some tracks through one of Miss Jean's flower-beds."

"Tracks!"

"Sure! Strange tracks. Man's tracks."

"What does that signify?"

"We ain't altogether certain. Carara says he seen a stranger hangin' around night before last, and jest now we found where a hoss had been picketed out in the ravine. Looks like he'd stood there more'n once."

"Why, this is decidedly mysterious."

"We figured we'd ought to tell you."

"It has nothing to do with me."

"I ain't sure. It looks to us like it's somebody from the Centipede. They're equal to any devilment."

Speed showed an utter lack of comprehension, so Willie explained.

"Understand, we've made this race pay or play. Mebbe they aim to cripple you."

"Me!" Speed started. "Good Heavens!"

"Oh, they'd do it quick enough! I wouldn't put it past 'em to drop a .45 through your winder if it could be done safe."

"Shoot me, you mean?"

"Allah!" said Glass, devoutly from his corner.

Stover and Willie nodded. "If I was you, I'd keep the lamp between me and the winder every night."

"Why, this is abominable!" exclaimed the young college man, stiffly. "I—I can't stand for this, it's getting too serious."

"There ain't nothin' to fear," said Willie, soothingly. "Remember, I told you at the start that we'd see there wasn't no crooked work done. Well, I'm goin' to ride herd on you, constant, Mr. Speed." He smiled in a manner to reassure. "If there's any shootin' comes off, I'll be in on it."

"S—say, what's to prevent us being murdered when we're out for a run?" queried Glass.

"Me!" declared the little man. "I'll saddle my bronc' an' lope along with you. We'll keep to the open country."

Instantly Speed saw the direful consequences of such a procedure, and summoned his courage to say: "No. It's very kind of you, but I shall give up training."

"What!"

"I mean training on the road. I—I'll run indoors."

"Not a bit like it," declared Stover. "You'll get your daily run if we have to lay off all the punchers on the place and put 'em on as a body-guard."

"But I don't want a body-guard!" cried the athlete desperately.

"We can't let you get hurt. You're worth too much to us."

"Larry and I will take a chance."

"Not for mine!" firmly declared the trainer. "I don't need no mineral in my system. I'm for the house."

"Then I shall run alone."

"You're game," said Willie admiringly, and his auditor breathed easier, "but we can't allow it."

"I—I'd rather risk my life than put you to so much trouble."

"It's only a pleasure."

"Nevertheless, I can't allow it. I'll run alone, if they kill me for it."

"Oh, they won't try to kill you. They'll probably shoot you in the legs. That's just as good, and it's a heap easier to get away with."

Speed felt his knee-caps twitching.

"I've got it!" said he at last. "I'll run at night!"

Stover hesitated thoughtfully. "I don't reckon you could do yourself justice that-away, but you might do your trainin' at daylight. The Centipede goes to work the same time we do, and the chances is your assassin won't miss his breakfast."

"Good! I—I'll do that!"

"I sure admire your courage, but if you see anything suspicious, let us know. We'll git 'em," said Willie.

"Thank you."

The two men went out, whereupon Glass chattered:

"W—what did I tell you? It's worse'n suicide to stick around this farm. I'm going to blow."

"Where are you going?"

"New York. Let's beat it!"

"Never!" exclaimed the college man, stubbornly. We'll hear from Covington before long. Besides, I can't leave until I get some money from home."

"Let's walk."

"Don't be a fool!"

"Then I've got to have a drink." Glass started for the living-quarters, but at the door ducked quickly out of sight.

"She's there!" he whispered tragically. "She seen me, too!"

Mariedetta was squatting in the shade opposite, her eyes fixed stolidly upon the training-quarters.

"Then you've got to lay low till she gives up," declared Wally. "We're in trouble enough as it is."

For nearly an hour the partners discussed the situation while the Mexican maid retained her position; then, when Glass was on the verge of making a desperate sally, Cloudy entered silently. Although this had been an unhappy morning for the trainer, here at least was one person of whom he had no fear, and his natural optimism being again to the fore, he greeted the Indian lightly.

"Well, how's the weather, Cloudy?"

"Mr. Cloudy to you," said the other. Both Glass and his protege stared. It was the first word the Indian had uttered since their arrival. Lawrence winked at his companion.

"All right, if you like it better. How's the weather, Mister Cloudy?" He snickered at his own joke, whereupon the aborigine turned upon him slowly, and said, in perfect English:

"Your humor is misplaced with me. Don't forget, Mr. Glass, that the one Yale football team you trained, I dropped a goal on from the forty-five-yard line."

Glass allowed his mouth to open in amazement. The day was replete with surprises.

"'96!" he said, while the light of understanding came over him. "You're Cloudy-but-the-Sun-Shines?"

"Yes—Carlisle." Cloudy threw back his head, and pointed with dignity to the flag of his Alma Mater hanging upon the wall.

"By Jove, I remember that!" exclaimed Speed.

"So will Yale so long as she lives," predicted the Indian, grimly. "You crippled me in the second half"—he stirred his withered leg—"but I dropped it on you; and—I have not forgotten." He ground the last sentence between his teeth.

"See here, Bo—Mr. Cloudy. You don't blame us for that?" Cloudy grunted, and threw a yellow envelope on the floor at Speed's feet. "There is something for you," said he, while his lips curled. He turned, and limped silently to the door.

"And I tried to kid him!" breathed Glass with disgust, when the visitor had gone. "I ain't been in right since Garfield was shot."

"It's a telegram from Covington!" cried Speed, tearing open the message. "At last!"

"Thank the Lord!" Glass started forward eagerly. "When'll he be here? Quick!" Then he paused. J. Wallingford Speed had gone deathly pale, and was reeling slightly. "What's wrong?"

The college man made uncertainly for his bed, murmuring incoherently:

"I—I'm sick! I'm sick, Larry!" He fell limply at full length, and groaned, "Call the race off!"

Glass snatched the missive from his employer's nerveless fingers, and read, with bulging eyes, as follows:

"J. WALLINGFORD SPEED, Flying Heart Ranch, Kidder, New Mexico:

"Don't tip off. Am in jail Omaha. Looks like ten days.

"CULVER COVINGTON."

The trainer uttered a cry like that of a wounded animal.

"Call it off, Larry," moaned the Hope of the Flying Heart. "I've been poisoned!"

"Poisoned, eh?" said the fat man, tremulously. "Poisoned! Nix! Not with me!" He walked firmly across the room, flung back the lid of

Speed's athletic trunk, and began to paw through it feverishly. One after another he selected three heavy sweaters, then laid strong hands upon his protege and jerked him to his feet. "Sick, eh? Here, get into these!"

"What do you mean, Lawrence?" inquired his victim.

"If you get sick, I die." Glass opened the first sweater, and half-smothered his protege with it. "Hurry up! You're going into training!"

CHAPTER XI

That was a terrible hour for J. Wallingford Speed. As for Larry, once he had grasped the full significance of the telegram, he became a different person. Some fierce electric charge wrought a chemical alteration in his every fibre; he became a domineering, iron-willed autocrat, obsessed by the one idea of his own preservation, and not hesitating to use physical force when force became necessary to lessen his peril.

Repeatedly Speed folded his arms over his stomach, rocked in the throes of anguish, and wailed that he was perishing of cramps; the trainer only snorted with derision. When he refused to don the clothes selected for him, Glass fell upon him like a raging grizzly.

"You won't, eh? We'll see!" Then Speed took refuge in anger, but the other cried:

"Never mind the hysterics, Bo. You're going to run off some blubber to-day."

"But I have to go riding!"

"Not a chance!"

"I tell you I'll run when I come back," maintained the youth, almost tearfully beseeching. "They're waiting for me."

"Let 'em gallop — you can run alongside."

"With all these sweaters? I'd have a sunstroke."

"It's the best thing for you. I never thought of that."

As Glass forced his protege toward the house, the other young people appeared clad for their excursion; their horses were tethered to the porch. And it was an ideal day for a ride — warm, bright, and inviting. Over to the northward the hills, mysteriously purple, invited exploration; to the south and east the golden prairie undulated gently into a hazy realm of infinite possibilities; the animals themselves turned friendly eyes upon their riders, champing and whinnying as if eager to bear them out into the distances.

"We are ready!" called Jean gayly.

"What in the world—" Helen paused at sight of the swathed figure. "Are you cold, Mr. Speed?"

"Climb on your horses and get a start," panted the burly trainer; "he's goin' to race you ten miles."

"I'm going to do nothing of the sort. I'm going to—"

But Glass jerked him violently, crying:

"And no talkin' to gals, neither. You're trainin'. Now, get a move!"

Speed halted stubbornly.

"Hit her up, Wally! G'wan, now—faster! No loafing, Bo, or I'll wallop you!" Nor did he cease until they both paused from exhaustion. Even then he would not allow his charge to do more than regain his breath before urging him onward.

"See here," Wally stormed at last, "what's the use? I can't—"

"What's the use? That's the use!" Glass pointed to the north, where a lone horseman was watching them from a knoll. "D'you know who that is?"

The rider was small and stoop-shouldered.

"Willie!"

"That's who."

"He's following us!"

With knees trembling beneath him Speed jogged feebly on down the road, Glass puffing at his heels.

When, after covering five miles, they finally returned to the Flying Heart, it was with difficulty that they could drag one foot after another. Wally Speed was drenched with perspiration, and Glass resembled nothing so much as a steaming pudding; rivulets of sweat ran down his neck, his face was purple, his lips swollen.

"Y-you'll have—to run alone—this afternoon," panted the tormentor.

"This afternoon? Haven't I run enough for—one day?" the victim pleaded. "Glass, old man, I—I'm all in, I tell you; I'm ready to die."

"Got to—fry off some more—leaf-lard," declared the trainer with vulgarity. He lumbered into the cook-house, radiating heat waves, puffing like a traction-engine, while his companion staggered to the gymnasium, and sank into a chair. A moment later he appeared with two bottles of beer, one glued to his lips. Both were evidently ice cold, judging from the fog that covered them.

Speed rose with a cry.

"Gee! That looks good!"

But the other, thrusting him aside without removing the neck of the bottle from his lips, gurgled:

"No booze, Wally! You're trainin'!"

"But I'm thirsty!" shouted the athlete, laying hands upon the full bottle, and trying to wrench it free.

"Have a little sense. If you're thirsty, hit the sink." Glass still maintained his hold, mumbling indistinctly: "Water's the worst thing in the world. Wait! I'll get you some."

He stepped into the bunk-room, to return an instant later with a cup half full. "Rinse out your mouth, and don't swallow it all."

"All! There isn't that much. Ugh! It's lukewarm. I want a bucket of ice-water—ice-water!"

"Nothing doing! I won't stand to have your epictetus chilled."

"My what?"

"Never mind now. Off with them clothes, and get under that shower. I guess it'll feel pretty good to-day."

Speed obeyed instructions sullenly, while his trainer, reclining in the cosey-corner, uncorked the second bottle. From behind the blanket curtains where the barrel stood, the former demanded:

"What did you mean by saying I'd have to run again this afternoon?"

"Starts!" said Glass, shortly.

"Starts?"

"Fast work. We been loafing so far; you got to get some ginger."

"Rats! What's the use?"

"No use at all. You couldn't outrun a steam-roller, but if you won't duck out, I've got to do my best. I'd as lief die of a gunshot-wound as starve to death in the desert."

"Do you suppose we could run away?"

"Could we!" Glass propped himself eagerly upon one elbow. "Leave it to me."

"No!" Wally resumed rubbing himself down. "I can't leave without looking like a quitter. Fresno would get her sure."

"What's the difference if you're astraddle of a cloud with a gold guitar in your lap?"

"Oh, they won't kill us."

"I tell you these cow-persons is desp'rate. If you stay here and run that race next Saturday, she'll tiptoe up on Sunday and put a rose in your hand, sure. I can see her now, all in black. Take it from me, Wally, we ain't goin' to have no luck in this thing."

"My dear fellow, the simplest way out of the difficulty is for me to injure myself—"

"Here!" Glass hopped to his feet and dove through the blankets. "None of that! Have a little regard for me. If you go lame it's my curtain."

All that day the trainer stayed close to his charge, never allowing him out of his sight, and when, late in the afternoon, Speed rebelled at the espionage, Glass merely shrugged his fat shoulders. "But I want to be alone—with her. Can't you see?"

"I can, but I won't. Go as far as you like. I'll close my eyes."

"Or I'll close them for you!" The lad scowled; his companion laughed mirthlessly.

"Don't start nothin' like that—I'd ruin you. Gals is bad for a man in trainin' anyhow."

"I suppose I'm not to see her—"

"You can see her, but I want to hear what you say to her. No emotion till after this race, Wally."

"You're an idiot! This whole affair is preposterous—ridiculous."

"And yet it don't make us laugh, does it?" Glass mocked.

"If these cowboys make me run that race, they'll be sorry—mark my words, they'll be sorry."

Speed lighted a cigarette and inhaled deeply, but only once. The other lunged at him with a cry and snatched it. "Give me that cigarette!"

"I've had enough of this foolishness," Wally stormed. "You are discharged!"

"I wish I was."

"You are!"

"Not!"

"I say you are fired!" Glass stared at him. "Oh, I mean it! I won't be bullied."

"Very well." Glass rose ponderously. "I'll wise up that queen of yours, Mr. Speed."

"You aren't going to talk to Miss Blake? Wait!" Speed wilted miserably. "She mustn't know. I—I hire you over again."

"Suit yourself."

"You see, don't you? My love for Helen is the only serious thing I ever experienced," said the boy. "I—can't lose her. You've got to help me out."

And so it was agreed.

That evening, when the clock struck nine, J. Wallingford Speed was ready and willing to drag himself off to bed, in spite of the knowledge that Fresno was waiting to take his place in the hammock. He was racked by a thousand pains, his muscles were sore, his back lame. He was consumed by a thirst which Glass stoutly refused to let him quench, and possessed by a fearful longing for a smoke. When he dozed off, regardless of the snores from the bunk-house adjoining, Berkeley Fresno's musical tenor was sounding in his ears. And Helen Blake was vaguely surprised. For the first time in their acquaintance Mr. Speed had yawned openly in her presence, and she wondered if he were tiring of her.

It seemed to Speed that he had barely closed his eyes when he felt a rough hand shaking him, and heard his trainer's voice calling, in a half-whisper: "Come on, Cull! Get up!"

When he turned over it was only to be shaken into complete wakefulness.

"Hurry up, it's daylight!"

"Where?"

"Come, now, you got to run five miles before breakfast!"

Speed sat up with a groan. "If I run five miles," he said, "I won't want any breakfast," and laid himself down again gratefully—he was very sore—whereat his companion fairly dragged him out of bed. As yet the room was black, although the windows were grayed by the first faint streaks of dawn. From the adjoining room came a chorus of distress: snores of every size, volume, and degree of intensity, from the last harrowing gasp of strangulation to the bold trumpetings of a bull moose. There were long drawn sighs, groans of torture, rumbling blasts. Speed shuddered.

"They sound like a troop of trained sea-lions," said he.

"Don't wake 'em up. Here!" Glass yawned widely, and tossed a bundle of sweaters at his companion.

"Ugh! These clothes are all wet and cold, and—it feels like blood!"

"Nothin' but the mornin' dew."

"It's perspiration."

"Well, a little sweat won't hurt you."

"Nasty word." Speed yawned in turn. "Perspiration! I can't wear wet clothes," and would have crept back into his bed.

This time Glass deposited him upon a stool beside the table, and then lighted a candle, by the sickly glare of which he selected a pair of running-shoes.

"Why didn't you leave me alone?" grumbled the younger man. "The only pleasure I get is in sleep—I forget things then."

"Yes," retorted the former, sarcastically, "and you also seem to forget that these are our last days among the living. Saturday the big thing comes off."

"Forget! I dreamed about it!" The boy sighed heavily. It was the hour in which hope reaches its lowest ebb and vitality is weakest. He was very cold and very miserable.

"You ain't got no edge on me," the other acknowledged, mournfully. "I'm too young to die, and that's a bet."

Suddenly the pandemonium in the bunk-house was pierced by the brazen jangle of an alarm-clock, whereat a sleepy voice cried:

"Cloudy, kill that damn clock!"

The Indian uttered some indistinguishable epithet, and the next instant there came a crash as the offending timepiece was hurled violently against the wall. In silence Glass shoved his unsteady victim ahead of him out into the dawn. In the east the sun was rising amid a riotous splendor. At any other time, under any other conditions, Speed could not have restrained his admiration, for the whole world was a glorious sparkling panoply of color. The tumbled masses of the hills were blazing at their crests, the valleys dark and cool. In the east the limb of the sun was just rearing itself, the air was heady with the scent of growing things, and so clear that the distances were magically shortened; a certain wild, intoxicating exuberance surcharged the out-of- doors. But to the stiff and wearied Eastern lad it was all cruelly mocking. When he halted listlessly to view its beauties he was goaded forward, ever forward, faster and faster, until finally, amid protests and sighs and complaining joints, he broke into a heavy, flat-footed jog-trot that jolted the artistic sense entirely out of him.

CHAPTER XII

It was usually a procedure not alone of difficulty but of diplomacy as well, to rout out the ranch-hands of the Flying Heart without engendering hostile relations that might bear fruit during the day. This morning Still Bill Stover had more than his customary share of trouble, for they seemed pessimistic.

Carara, for instance, breathed a Spanish oath as he combed his hair, and when the foreman inquired the reason, replied:

"I don' sleep good. I been t'ink mebbe I lose my saddle on this footrace."

Cloudy, whose toilet was much less intricate, grunted from the shadows:

"I thought I heard that phonograph all night."

"It was the Natif Son singin' to his gal," explained one of the hands. "He's gettin' on my nerves, too. If he wasn't a friend of the boss, I'd sure take a surcingle and abate him considerable."

"Vat you t'ank? I dream' Mr. Speed is ron avay an' broke his leg," volunteered Murphy, the Swede, whose name New Mexico had shortened from Bjorth Kjelliser.

"Run away?"

"Ya-as! I dream' he's out for little ron ven piece of noosepaper blow up in his face an' mak' him ron avay, yust same as horse. He snort an' yump, an' ron till he step in prairie-dog hole and broke his leg."

"Strange!" said Willie.

"What?"

"My rest was fitful and disturbed and peopled by strange fancies a whole lot. I dreamp' he throwed the race!"

A chorus of oaths from the bunks.

"What did you do?" inquired Stover.

"I woke up, all of a tremble, with a gun in each hand."

"I don't take no stock in dreams whatever," said some one.

"Well, I'm the last person in the world to be superstitious," Still Bill observed, "but I've had sim'lar visions lately."

"Maybe it's a om-en."

"What is a om-en?" Carara inquired.

"A om-en," explained Willie, "is a kind of a nut. Salted om-ens is served at swell restaurants with the soup."

In the midst of it Joy, the cook, appeared in the doorway, and spoke in his gentle, ingratiating tones:

"Morning, gel'mum! I see 'im again."

"Who?"

"No savvy who; stlange man! I go down to spling-house for bucket water; see 'im lide 'way. Velly stlange!"

"I bet it's Gallagher."

"Vat you tank he vants?" queried Murphy.

"He's layin' to get a shot at our runner," declared Stover, while Mr. Cloudy, forgetting his Indian reserve, explained in classic English his own theory of the nocturnal visits. "Do you remember Humpy Joe? Well, they didn't cripple him, but he lost. I don't think Gallagher would injure Mr. Speed, but—he might—bribe him."

"Caramba!" exclaimed the Mexican.

"God 'lmighty!" Willie cried, in shocked accents.

"I believe you're right, but"—Stover meditated briefly before announcing with determination—"we'll do a little night-ridin' ourselves. Willie, you watch this young feller daytimes, and the rest of us'll take turns at night. An' don't lose sight of the fat man, neither—he might carry notes. If you don't like the looks of things—you know what cards to draw."

"Sixes," murmured the near-sighted cow-man. "Don't worry."

"If you see anything suspicious, burn it up. And we'll take a shot at anything we see movin' after 9 P.M."

Then Berkeley Fresno came hurriedly into the bunk-house with a very cheery "Good-morning! I'm glad I found you up and doing," he said blithely. "I thought of something in my sleep." It was evident that the speaker had been in more than ordinary haste to make his discovery known, for underneath his coat he still wore his pajama shirt, and his hair was unbrushed.

"What is it?"

"Your man Speed isn't taking care of himself."

"What did I tell you?" said Willie to his companions.

"It seems to me that in justice to you boys he shouldn't act this way," Fresno ran on. "Now, for instance, the water in his shower-bath is tepid."

There was an instant's silence before Stover inquired, with ominous restraint:

"Who's been monkeying with it?"

"It's warm!"

"Oh!" It was a sigh of relief.

"A man can't get in shape taking warm shower-baths. Warm water weakens a person."

"Mebbe you-all will listen to me next time!" again cried Willie, triumphantly. "I said at the start that a bath never helped nobody. When they're hot they saps a man's courage, and when they're cold they—"

"No, no! You don't understand! For an athlete the bath ought to be cold—the colder the better. It's the shock that hardens a fellow."

"Has he weakened himself much?" inquired the foreman.

"Undoubtedly, but—"

"What?"

"If we only had some ice—"

"We got ice; plenty of it. We got a load from the railroad yesterday."

"Then our only chance to save him is to fill the barrel quickly. We must freeze him, and freeze him well, before it is too late! By Jove! I'm glad I thought of it!"

Stover turned to his men. "Four of you-all hustle up a couple hundred pounds of that ice pronto! Crack it, an' fill the bar'l." There was a scramble for the door.

"And there's something else, too," went on Berkeley. "He's being fed wrong for his last days of training. The idea of a man eating lamb-chops, fried eggs, oatmeal, and all that debilitating stuff! Those girls overload his stomach. Why, he ought to have something to make him strong—fierce!"

"Name it," said Willie, shortly.

"Something like—like—bear meat."

"We ain't got no bear." Willie looked chagrined.

"This ain't their habitat," added Stover apologetically.

"Well, he ought to have meat, and it ought to be wild—raw, if possible."

"There ain't nothin' wilder 'n a long-horn. We can git him a steer."

"You are sure the meat isn't too tender?"

"It's tougher 'n a night in jail."

"There ain't no sausage-mill that'll dent it."

"Good! The rarer it is the better. Some raw eggs and a good strong vegetable—"

"Onions?"

"Fine! We'll save him yet!"

"We'll get the grub."

"And he'll eat it!" Willie nodded firmly.

Stover issued another order, this time to Carara. "You 'n Cloudy butcher the wildest four-year-old you can find. If you can't get close enough to rope him, shoot him, and bring in a hind quarter. It's got to be here in time for breakfast."

"Si, Senor!" The Mexican picked up his lariat; the Indian took a Winchester from an upper bunk and filled it with cartridges.

"Of course, he'll have to eat out here; they spoil him up at the house."

"Sure thing!"

"I'd hate to see him lose; it would be a terrible blow to Miss Blake." Fresno shook his head doubtfully.

"What about us?"

"Oh, you can stand it—but she's a girl. Ah, well," the speaker sighed, "I hope nothing occurs between now and Saturday to prevent his running."

"It won't," Stover grimly assured the Californian. "Nothin' whatever is goin' to occur."

"He was speaking yesterday about the possibility of some business engagement—"

The small man in glasses interrupted. "Nothin' but death shall take him from us, Mr. Fresno."

"If I think of anything else," offered Berkeley, kindly, "I'll tell you."

"We wish you would."

Fresno returned to the house, humming cheerily. It was still an hour until his breakfast-time, but he had accomplished much. In the midst of his meditation he came upon Miss Blake emerging upon the rear porch.

"Good-morning!" he cried. She started a trifle guiltily. "What are you doing at this hour?"

"Oh, I just love the morning air," she answered. "And you?"

"Same here! 'Honesty goes to bed early, and industry rises betimes.' That's me!"

"Then you have been working?"

Fresno nodded. He was looking at four cowboys who were entering the gymnasium, staggering beneath dripping gunny-sacks. Then he turned his gaze searchingly upon the girl.

"Were you looking for Speed?" he asked accusingly. "The idea!" Miss Blake flushed faintly.

"If you are, he has gone for a run. I dearly love to see him get up early and run, he enjoys it so. To give pleasure to others is one of my constant aims. That is why I learned to sing." "I have been baking a cake," said Helen, displaying the traces of her occupation upon hands, arms, and apron, while Fresno, at sight of the blue apron tied at her throat and waist, felt that he himself was as dough in her hands. "I had a dreadful time to make it rise."

"Early rising is always unpopular."

"How clever you are this morning."

"If I were a cake I would rise at your lightest word."

"The cook said it wouldn't be fit to eat," declared Helen.

"Jealousy! She hadn't been up long."

"And I did leave a lot of dishes to wash after I had finished," Miss Blake admitted.

"I should love to eat your cooking."

"Once in a while, perhaps, but not every day."

"Every day—always and always. You know what I-mean, Miss Blake— Helen!" The young man bent a lover's gaze upon his companion until he detected her eyes fastened with startled inquiry upon his toilet. Remembering, he buttoned his coat, but ran on. "This is the first chance I've had to see you alone since Speed arrived. There's something I want to ask you."

"I—I know what it is," stammered Helen. "You want me to let you sing again. Please do. I love morning music—and your voice is so tender."

"Life," said Berkeley, "is one sweet—"

"What is going on here?" demanded a voice behind them, and Mrs. Keap came out upon the porch, eying the pair suspiciously. It was evident that she, like Fresno, had dressed hurriedly.

"Mr. Fresno is going to sing to us," explained the younger girl, quickly.

"Really?"

"I am like the bird that greets the morn with song," laughed the tenor, awkwardly.

"What are you going to sing?" demanded the chaperon, still suspiciously. "Dearie."

"Don't you know any other song?"

"Oh yes, but they are all sad."

"I'm getting a trifle tired of Dearie, let's have one of the others." Mrs. Keap turned her eyes anxiously toward the training-quarters, and it was patent that she had not counted upon this encounter. Noting her lack of ease, Fresno said hopefully:

"If you are going for a walk, I'll sing for you at some other time."

"Is Mr. Speed up yet?"

"Up and gone. He'll be back soon."

Then Mrs. Keap sank into the hammock, and with something like resignation, said:

"Proceed with the song."

Along the road toward the ranch buildings plodded two dusty pedestrians, one a blond youth bundled thickly in sweaters, the other a fat man who rolled heavily, and paused now and then to mop his purple face. Both were dripping as if from an immersion, while the air about the latter vibrated with heat waves. They both stumbled as they walked, and it was only by the strongest effort of will that they propelled themselves. As they neared the corner of the big, low-lying ranch-house, already reflecting the hot glare of the morning sun, a man's clear tenor voice came to them.

"The volley was fired at sunrise,
Just at the break of day" —

"Did you get that?" one of the two exclaimed hoarsely. "They're practising a death-march, and it's ours."

"And as the echoes lingered,
His soul had passed away."

"That's you, Wally!" wheezed the trainer.

"Into the arms of his Maker,
There to learn his fate" —

Speed broke into a run.

"A tear, a sigh, a last 'Good-bye' —
The pardon came too late."

"Here, what are you singing about?" angrily protested Speed, as he rounded into view.

"Oh, it's Mr. Speed!"

"Good-morning!" chorused Helen and the chaperon.

"Welcome to our city!" Fresno greeted.

Glass tottered to the steps. "Them songs," he puffed, "is bad for a man when he's trainin'; they get him all worked up."

"We had no idea you would be back so soon," apologized Helen.

"Soon!" Speed measured the distance to a wicker chair, gave it up, and sank beside his trainer. "We left yesterday! We've run miles and miles and miles!"

"You can't be in very good shape," volunteered the singer.

"Oh, is that so?" Glass retorted. "I say he's great. He got my goat—and I'm some runner."

"And I'd be obliged to you if you'd cut out those deeply appealing songs." Speed glowered at his rival. It was Helen who hastened to smooth things.

"It's all my fault. I asked Mr. Fresno to sing something new."

"Bah! That was written by William Cromwell."

"No more of them battle-hymns," Glass ordered. "They don't do Mr. Speed no good."

"All I want is a drink," panted that youthful athlete, and Helen rose quickly, saying that she would bring ice-water.

But the trainer barked, sharply: "Nix! I've told you that twenty times, Wally. It'll put hob-nails in your liver." He rose with difficulty, swaying upon his feet, and where he had sat was a large, irregular shaped, sweat-dampened area. "Come on! Don't get chilled."

"I'd give twenty dollars for a good chill!" exclaimed the overheated college man longingly.

"I would like to see you a moment, Mr. Speed." Roberta rose from the hammock.

"Oh, and I've forgotten my—" Helen checked her words with a startled glance toward the kitchen. "It will be burned to a crisp." She hastened down the porch, and Fresno followed, while Speed looked after them.

"He must be an awful nuisance to a nice girl. Think of a fat, sandy-haired husband in a five-room flat with pink wall-paper and a colored janitor. Run along, Muldoon," to Glass, "I'll be with you in a moment."

When the trainer had waddled out of hearing, Mrs. Keap inquired, eagerly:

"Have you heard from Culver?"

"Didn't you know about it?" Speed swallowed.

Roberta shook her dark head.

"He's in—he's detained at Omaha for ten days. I fixed it."

The overwrought widow dropped back into the hammock, crying weakly:

"Oh, you dear, good boy!"

"Yes, I'm all of that. I—I suppose I'd be missed if anything happened to me!"

"How ever did you manage it?"

"Never mind the details. It took some ingenuity."

Mrs. Keap wrung her hands. "I was so terribly frightened! You see, Jack will be back to-morrow, and I—was afraid—"

There was a call from Glass from the training-quarters.

"How can I ever do enough for you? You have averted a tragedy!"

"Don't let Helen know, that's all. If she thought I'd been the head yeller—"

"I won't breathe a word, and I hope you win the race for her sake."

Mrs. Keap pressed the hand of her deliverer, who trudged his lonely way toward the gymnasium, where Glass was saying:

"'The volley was fired at sunrise.' That means Saturday, Bo."

"Larry, you're the best crepe-hanger of your weight in the world."

Larry bent a look of open disgust upon his employer.

"And you're a good runner, you are," said he. "Why, I beat you this morning."

The younger man glanced up hopefully. "Couldn't you beat this cook?"

"You're the only man in this world I can outrun."

"'A tear, a sigh, a last good-bye.'"

"Shut up!"

As Glass consented to do this, the speaker mused, bitterly, "'Early to bed and early to rise.' I wish I had the night- watchman who wrote those words."

"Didn't you never see the sun rise before?"

"Certainly not. I don't stay up that late."

"Well, ain't it beautiful!" The stout man turned admiring eyes to the eastward, and his husky voice softened. "All them colors and tints and shades and stuff! And New York on the other end!"

"I'm too tired to see beauty in anything." As if mindful of a neglected duty, Glass turned upon him. "What are you waiting for? Get those dog-beds off your back." He seized the slack of a sweater and gave it a jerk.

"Don't be so rough; I'll come. You might care to remember you're working for me."

"I am working"—Glass dragged his protege about the room regardless of complaints that were muffled by the thickness of the sweaters—"for my life, and I'll be out of a job Saturday. Now, get under that shower!"

CHAPTER XIII

"Do you know, Larry, I'm beginning to like these warm showers; they rest me." As he spoke, Wally took his place beneath the barrel and pulled the cord that connected with the nozzle. The next instant he uttered a piercing shriek and leaped from beneath the apparatus, upsetting Glass, who rose in time to fling his charge back into the deluge.

"Let me out!" yelled the athlete, and made another dash, at which his guardian bellowed:

"Stand still, or I'll wallop you! What's got into you, anyhow?"

The heads of Stover and Willie, thrust through the door, nodded with gratification.

"It's got him livened up considerable," quoth the former. "Listen to that!" It seemed that a battle must be in progress behind the screen, for, mingled with the gasping screams of the athlete and the hoarse commands of the trainer, came sounds of physical contact. The barrel rocked upon its scaffold, the curtains swayed and flapped violently.

"Stand still!"

"It's—it's as c-c-cold as ice!"

"Nix! You're overheated, that's all."

"Ow-w-w! Ooo-h-h! I'm dying!"

"It'll do you good."

"He's certainly trainin' him some," said Stover.

"Larry, I've got a cramp!"

"It did harden him," acknowledged Willie.

"What's wrong with you, anyhow?" demanded Glass.

"It's not me, it's the w-w-water!"

Evidently Speed made a frantic lunge here and escaped, for the flow of water ceased.

"It froze d-d-during the night. Oh-h! I'm cold!"

"Cold, eh? Get onto that rubbing-board; I'll warm you."

An instant later the cow-men heard the sounds of a violent slapping mingled with groans.

"Go easy, I say! I'll be black and blue all—LOOK OUT!—not so much in one spot! Ow!"

"Turn over!"

"He's spankin' him," said Stover admiringly.

Again the spatting arose, this time like the sound of a musketry fusilade, during which Berkeley Fresno entered by the other door.

"Don't be so brutal!" wailed the patient to his masseur.

"I'm pretty near through. There! Now get up and dress," ordered the trainer, who, pushing his way out through the blankets, halted at sight of the onlookers.

"How is he?" demanded Stover.

"He—he's trained to the minute. I'm doin' my share, gents."

"Sounds that way," acknowledged Stover's companion. "Say, does it look like we'd win?"

"Well, he just breezed a mile in forty, with his mouth open."

"A mile?" Fresno queried.

"Yes, a regular mile—seven thousand five hundred and thirty feet."

"Is 'forty' good?" queried Willie.

"Good? Why, Salvator never worked no faster. Here he is now—look for yourselves."

Speed appeared, partly clad, and glowing with a rich salmon pink.

"Good-morning," said Fresno politely. "I came in to see how you liked the cold water."

"So that was one of your California jokes, eh? Well, I'll—"

Speed moved ominously in the direction of the tenor, but Willie checked him.

"We put the ice in that bar'l, Mr. Speed."

"You!"

Willie and Stover nodded.

"Then let me tell you I expect to have pneumonia from that bath." The young man coughed hollowly. "That's the way I caught it once before, and it wouldn't surprise me a bit if I'd be too sick to run by Saturday."

"Oh no; you don't get pneumony but once."

"And, besides," Fresno added, "it wouldn't have time to show up by Saturday."

"Get that ice-chest out of my room, that's all; it makes the air damp."

"No indeed!" said Still Bill. "We're goin' to see that you use it reg'lar." Then of Glass he inquired: "What do you do to him next?"

"I give him a nerve treatment. A jack-rabbit jumped at him this morning and he bolted to the outside fence." Larry forced his employer to a seat, then, securing a firm hold of the flesh, began to discourse learnedly upon anatomy and hygiene, the while his victim writhed. It was evident that the cattle-men were intensely interested. "Well, sir, when I first got him his sploven was in terrible shape," said Larry. "In fact, I never saw such a —"

"What was in terrible shape?" ventured the tenor. "His sploven."

"Sploven! Is that a locality or a beverage?"

Glass glowered at the cause of the interruption. "It's a nerve-centre, of course!" Then to the others, he ran on, glibly: "The treatment was simple, but it took time. You see, I had to first trace his bedildo to its source, like this." He thrust a finger into Wally's back and ploughed a furrow upward. "You see?" He paused, triumphantly. "A fore-shortened bedildo! It ain't well yet."

"Can a man run fast with one of them?" inquired Willie.

"Certainly, cer-tain-ly — provided, of course, that the percentage of spelldiffer in the blood offsets it."

Both cowboys came closer now, and hung eagerly upon every word.

"And does it do—that?" they questioned, while Fresno suggested that it was not easy to tell without bleeding the patient.

"No, no! You can hear the spelldiffers." Glass motioned to Willie.

"Put your ear to his chest. Hear anything?"

"Hearts poundin' like a calf's at a brandin'."

"Which proves it!" proudly asserted the trainer. "Barrin' accidents, Mr. Speed will be in the pink of condition by Saturday."

The cow-men beamed benignantly.

"That's fine!"

"We are sure pleased, and we've got something for you, Mr. Speed. Come on, Mr. Fresno, and give us a hand. We'll bring it in."

"It's a present!" exclaimed the athlete, brightly, when the three had gone out. "They seem more friendly this morning."

"Yes!" Glass laughed, mirthlessly. "They think you're going to win."

"Well, how do you know I can't win? You never saw this cook run."

"I don't have to; I've seen you."

"Just the same, I'm in pretty good shape. Maybe I could run if I really tried."

"Send yourself along, Kid. It won't harm you none." The speaker fanned himself, and took a seat in the cosey-corner.

"Ah! Here they come, bearing gifts." Speed rose in pleased expectancy. "I wonder what it can be?"

The three who had just left re-entered the room, carrying a trayload of thick railroad crockery.

"We've brought your breakfast to you," explained Stover. "We'd like you to eat alone till after the race." Still Bill began to whittle what appeared to be a blood-rare piece of flesh, while Willie awkwardly arranged the dishes.

"You want me to eat as well as sleep here?"

"Exactly."

"Oh, I can't do that! I'm sorry, but—"

"Don't make us insist." Willie looked up from his tray, and Glass raised a moist hand and said:

"Don't make 'em insist."

With fascinated stare Speed drew nearer to Stover and examined the meat bone.

"Why—why, that's raw!" he exclaimed.

"Does look rar'," agreed the foreman.

"Then take it out and build a fire under it. I'll consent to eat here, but I won't turn cannibal, even to please you."

"I'm sorry." Stover did not interrupt his carving.

"Your diet ain't been right," explained Willie. "You ain't wild enough to suit us."

Speed searched one serious face, then another. Fresno was nodding approval, his countenance impassive.

"Is this a joke?"

"We ain't never joked with you yit, have we?"

"No. But—"

"This breakfast goes as she lays!"

Glass broke abruptly into smothered merriment. "When I laugh nowadays it's a funny joke," he giggled.

That grown men could be so stupid was unbelievable, and Wally, seeing himself the object of a senseless prank, was roused to anger.

"Lawrence, get my coat," said he. "I've been bullied enough; I'm going up to the house." When Stover only continued whittling methodically, he burst out: "Stop honing that shin-bone! If you like it you can eat it! I'm going now to swallow a stack of hot cakes with maple syrup!"

"Mr. Speed," Willie impaled him with a steady glare, "you'll eat what we tell you to, and nothin' else! If we say 'grass,' grass it'll be. You're goin' to beat one Skinner if it takes a human life. And if that life happens to be yours, you got nobody but yourself to blame."

"Indeed!"

"You heard me! I've been set to ride herd on you daytimes, the other boys'll guard you nights. We been double-crossed once—it won't happen again."

"Then it amounts to this, does it: I'm your prisoner?"

"More of a prized possession," offered Stover. "If you ain't got the loy'lty to stand by us, we got to make you! This diet is part of the programme. Now if you think beef is too hearty for this time of day, tear into them eggs."

"You intend to make me eat this disgusting stuff, whether I want to or not?" Even yet the youth could not convince himself that this was other than a joke.

"No." Willie shook his head. "We just aim to make you want to eat it."

Then Larry Glass made his fatal mistake.

"Say, why don't you let Mr. Speed buy you a new phonograph, and call the race off?" he inquired.

Stover, stricken dumb, paused, knife in hand; Willie stared as if bereft of motion. Then the former spoke slowly. "Looks like we'd ought to smoke up this fat party, Will."

Willie nodded, and Glass realized that the little man's steel-blue eyes were riveted balefully upon him.

"I've had a hunch it would come to that," the near-sighted one replied. "Every time I look at him I see a bleedin' bullet-hole in his abominable regions, about here." He laid a finger upon his stomach, and Glass felt a darting pain at precisely the same spot. It was as agonizing as if Willie's spectacles were huge burning-glasses focussing the rays of a tropic sun upon his bare flesh. He folded protecting hands over the threatened region and backed toward the prayer-rug, mumbling "Allah! Allah!" No matter whither he shifted, the eyes bored into him.

"That's where you hit the gambler at Ogden," he heard Stover say — it might have been from a great distance — "but I aim for the bridge of the nose."

"The belly ain't so sudden as the eye-socket, but it's more lingerin', and a heap painfuller," explained the gun man, and Speed was moved to sympathy.

"Larry only wanted to please you — eh, Larry?" he said, nervously, but Glass made no reply. His distended orbs were frozen upon Willie. It was doubtful if he even heard.

"Our honor ain't for sale," Still Bill declared.

Here Berkeley Fresno spoke. "Of course not. And you mustn't think that Speed is trying to get out of the race. He wants to run! And if anything happened to prevent his running he'd be broken-hearted, I know he would!"

Willie's hypnotic eye left the trainer's abdomen and travelled slowly to Speed.

"What could happen?" questioned he.

"N-nothing that I know of."

"You don't aim to leave?"

"Certainly not."

"Oh, you fellows take it too seriously," Fresno offered carelessly. "He might have to."

Willie's upper lip drew back, showing his yellow teeth.

"They don't sell no railroad tickets before Saturday, and the walkin' is bad. There's your breakfast, Mr. Speed. When you've et your fill, you better rest. And don't talk to them ladies, neither; it spoils your train of thought!"

CHAPTER XIV

Now that the possibility of escape from the Flying Heart was cut off, the young man felt agonizing regret that he had not yielded to his trainer's earlier importunities and taken refuge in flight while there was yet time. It would have been undignified, perhaps; but once away from these single-minded cattle-men, his life would have been safe at least, and he could have trusted his ingenuity to reinstate him in Miss Blake's good graces. Everything was too late now. Even if he made a clean breast of the whole affair to Jean, or to her brother when he arrived, what good would that do? He doubted Jack's ability to save him, in the light of what had just passed; for men like Willie cared nothing for the orders of the person whose pay-roll they chanced to grace. And Willie was not alone, either; the rest of the crew were equally desperate. What heed would these nomads pay to Jack Chapin's commands, once they learned the truth? They were Arabs who owed allegiance to no one but themselves, the country was wild, the law was feeble, it was twenty miles to the railroad! And, besides, the thought of confession was abhorrent. Physical injury, no matter how severe, was infinitely preferable to Helen Blake's disdain. He cast about desperately for some saving loophole, but found himself trapped — completely, hopelessly trapped.

There were still, however, two days of grace, and to youth two days is an eternity. Therefore, he closed his eyes and trusted to the unexpected. How the unexpected could get past that grim, watchful sentry just outside the door he could not imagine, but when the breakfast-bell reminded him of his hunger, he banished his fears for the sake of the edibles his custodians had served.

"Don't you want anything to eat?" he inquired, when Larry made no move to depart for the cook-house.

"No."

"Not hungry, eh?"

"I'm hungry enough to eat a plush cushion, but—"

"What?"

"Mary!"

"Mariedetta?"

"Sure. She's been chasin' me again. If somebody don't side-track that Cuban, I'll have to lick Carara." He sighed. "I told you we'd ought to tin-can it out of here. Now it's too late."

Willie thrust his head in through the open window, inquiring, "Well, how's the breakfast goin'?" and withdrew, humming a favorite song:

"'Sam Bass was born in Indiany;
It was his natif home.
At the early age of seventeen
Young Sam commenced to roam.'"

"Fine voice!" said Lawrence, with a shudder.

It was perhaps a half-hour later that Helen Blake came tripping into the gymnasium, radiant, sparkling, her crisp white dress touched here and there with blue that matched her eyes, in her hands a sunshade, a novel, and a mysterious little bundle.

"We were so sorry to lose you at breakfast," she began.

Wally led her to the cosey-corner, and seated himself beside her.

"I suppose it is a part of this horrid training. I would never have mentioned that foot-race if I had dreamed it would be like this."

Here at least was a soul that sympathized.

"The only hardship is not to see you," he declared softly.

Miss Blake dropped her eyes.

"I thought you might like to go walking; it's a gorgeous morning. You see, I've brought a book to read to you while you rest—you must be tired after your run."

"I am, and I will. This is awfully good of you, Miss Blake." Speed rose, overwhelmed with joy, but the look of Glass was not to be passed by. "I-I'm afraid it's impossible, however." The blue eyes flew open in astonishment. "Why?" the girl questioned.

"They won't let me. I—I'm supposed to keep to myself."

"They? Who?"

"Glass."

Miss Blake turned indignantly upon Larry. "Do you mean to say Mr. Speed can't go walking with me?"

"I never said nothing of the sort," declared the trainer. "He can go if he wants to."

"Just the same, I—oughtn't to do it. There is a strict routine—"

A lift of the brows and a courteous smile proclaimed Miss Blake's perfect indifference to the subject, just as Willie sauntered past the open window and spoke to Glass beneath his breath:

"Git her out!"

"I'm so sorry. May I show you a surprise I brought for you?" She unwrapped her parcel, and proudly displayed a pallid, anaemic cake garlanded with wild flowers.

Speed was honestly overcome. "For me?"

"For you. It isn't even cold yet, see! I made it before breakfast, and it looks even better than the one I baked at school!"

"That's what I call fine," declared the youth. "By Jove! and I'm so fond of cake!"

"Have a care!" breathed Larry, rising nervously, but Speed paid no attention.

"Break it with your own hands, please. Besides, it's too hot to cut."

Miss Blake broke it with her own hands, during which operation the brown face of the man outside reappeared in the window. At sight of the cake he spoke sharply, and Lawrence lumbered swiftly across the floor and laid a heavy hand upon the cake.

"Mr. Speed!" he cried warningly.

"Here, take your foot off my angel-food!" fiercely ordered the youth. But the other was like adamant.

"Bo, you are about to contest for the honor of this ranch! That cake will make a bum of you!"

"Oh—h!" gasped the author of the delicacy. "Stop before it is too late!" Glass held his hungry employer at a distance, striving to make known by a wink the necessity of his act.

"There is absolutely nothing in my cake to injure any one," Helen objected loyally, with lifted chin; whereupon the corpulent trainer turned to her and said:

"Cake would crab any athlete. Cake and gals is the limit."

"Really! I had no idea I was the least bit dangerous." Miss Blake, turning to her host, smiled frigidly. "I'm so sorry I intruded."

"Now don't say that!" Speed strove to detain her. "Please don't be offended — I just have to train!"

"Of course. And will you pardon me for interrupting your routine? You see, I had no idea I wasn't wanted."

"But you are, and I do want you! I — "

"Good-bye!" She nodded pleasantly at the door, and left her lover staring after her.

When she had gone, he cried, in a trembling voice: "You're a fine yap, you are! She got up early to do something nice for me, and you insulted her! You wouldn't even let me sit and hold her hand!"

"No palm-readin'." Speed turned to behold his trainer ravenously devouring the cake, and dashed to its rescue.

"It's heavier than a frog full of buckshot. You won't like it, Cul."

"It's perfectly delicious!" came the choking answer.

"Then get back of them curtains. Willie'd shoot on sight."

All that morning the prisoner idled about the premises, followed at a distance by his guard. Wherever he went he seemed to see the sun flash defiance from the polished surface of those lenses, and while he was allowed a certain liberty, he knew full well that this espionage would never cease, night or day, until — what? He could not bear to read the future; anything seemed possible. Time and again he cursed that spirit of braggadocio, that thoughtless lack of moral scruple, which had led him into this predicament. He vowed that he was done with false pretences; henceforth the strictest probity should be his. No more false poses. Praise won by dissimulation and deceit was empty, anyhow, and did he escape this once, henceforth the world should know J. Wallingford Speed for what he was — an average individual, with no uncommon gifts of mind or body, courage or ability.

Yet it was small comfort to realize that he was getting his just deserts, and it likewise availed little to anathematize Fresno as the cause of his misfortune.

At noon Wally went through the mockery of a second blood-rare meal, with no cake to follow, and that afternoon Glass dragged him out under the hot sun, and made him sprint until he was ready to drop from exhaustion. His supper was wretched, and his fatigue so great that he fell asleep at Miss Blake's side during the evening. With the first hint of dawn he was up again, and Friday noon found him utterly hopeless, when, true to his prediction, the unexpected happened. In one moment he was raised from the blackest depths to the wildest transports of delight. It came in the shape of a telegram which Jean summoned him to the house to receive. He wondered listlessly as he opened the message, then started as if disbelieving his eyes; the marks of a wild emotion spread over his features, he burst into shrill, hysterical laughter.

"Do tell us!" begged Roberta.

"Covington—Covington is coming!" Wally felt his head whirl, and failed to note the chaperon's cry of surprise and see the paling of her cheeks. "Covington is coming! Don't you understand?" he shouted. After all, the gods were not deaf! Good old Culver, who had never failed him, was coming as a deliverer.

Even in the face of his extraordinary outburst the attention of the beholders was drawn to Lawrence Glass, who caused the porch to shake beneath his feet; who galloped to his employer, and, seizing him by the hands, capered about like a hippopotamus.

"I told you 'Allah' was some guy," he wheezed. "When does Covington arrive?" Wally reread the message. "It says 'Noon Friday.' Why, that's to-day! He's here now!"

"'Rah! 'Rah! 'Rah! Covington!" bellowed the trainer, and Mrs. Keap sank to a seat with a stifled moan.

"Why all the 'Oh joy! Oh, rapture!' stuff?" questioned Berkeley Fresno.

"As Socrates, the Hemlock Kid, would put it, 'Snatched from the shadow of the grave,'" quoth Glass, then paused abruptly. "Say, you don't think nothin' could happen to him on the way over from the depot?"

"I'm so sorry we didn't know in time to meet him," lamented Miss Chapin.

"And I could have run over to the railroad to bid him welcome," laughed Speed. "Twenty miles would do me good."

Still Bill and Willie approached the gallery curiously, and in subdued tones inquired:

"What's the matter, Mr. Speed?"

"You ain't been summoned away?" Willie stared questioningly upward. "No, no! My running partner is on his way here, that's all."

"Running pardner?"

"Culver Covington."

"Oh, we was afraid something had happened. You see, Gabby Gallagher has just blowed in from the Centipede to raise our bets."

"We think it's a bluff, and we'd like to call him."

"Do so, by all means!" cried the excited athlete. "Come on, let's all talk to him!"

The entire party, with the exception of Mrs. Keap, trooped down from the porch and followed the foreman out toward the sheds, where, in the midst of a crowd of ranch-hands, a burly, loud-voiced Texan was discoursing.

"I do wish Jack were here," said Jean nervously, on the way.

Gabby Gallagher seemed a fitting leader for such a desperate crew as that of the Centipede, for he was the hardest-looking citizen the Easterners had beheld thus far. He was thickset, and burned to the color of a ripe olive; his long, drooping mustaches, tobacco-stained at the centre, were bleached at the extremities to a hempen hue. His bristly hair was cut short, and stood aggressively erect upon a bullet head, his clothes were soiled and greasy beneath a gray coating of dust. A pair of alert, lead-blue eyes and a certain facility of movement belied the drawl that marked his nativity. He removed his hat and bowed at sight of Miss Chapin.

"Good-evenin', Miss Jean!" said he. "I hope I find y'all well."

"Quite well, Gallagher. And you?"

"Tol'able, thank you."

"These are my friends from the East."

The Centipede foreman ran his eyes coldly over Jean's companions until they rested upon Speed, where they remained. He shifted a lump in his cheek, spat dexterously, and directed his remark at the Yale man.

"I rode over to see if y'all would like to lay a little mo' on this y'ere foot-race. I allow you are the unknown?"

Speed nodded, and Stover took occasion to remark: "Them's our inclinations, but we've about gone our limit."

"I don't blame you none," said Gallagher, allowing his gaze to rove slowly from top to toe of the Eastern lad. "No, I cain't blame you none whatever. But I'm terrible grieved at them tidin's. Though we Centipede punchers has ever considered y'all a cheap an' poverty-ridden outfit, we gives you credit for bein' game, till now." He spat for a second time, and regarded Stover scornfully.

A murmur ran through the cowboys.

"We are game," retorted Stover, "and for your own good don't allow no belief to the contrary to become a superstition." Of a sudden the gangling, spineless foreman had grown taut and forceful, his long face was hard.

"Don't let a Centipede bluff you!" exclaimed Speed. "Cover anything they offer—give 'em odds. Anything you don't want, I'll take, pay or play, money at the tape. We can't lose."

"I got no more money," said Carara, removing his handsome bespangled hat, "but I bet my sombrero. 'E's wort' two hondred pesos."

Murphy, the Swede, followed quickly:

"Aye ban' send may vages home to may ole' moder, but aye skall bat you some."

"Haven't you boys risked enough already?" ventured Miss Chapin. "Remember, it will go pretty hard with the losers."

"Harder the better," came a voice.

"Y'all don't have to bet, jest because I'm h'yar," gibed Gallagher.

"God! I wish I was rich!" exclaimed Willie.

But Miss Chapin persisted. "You are two months overdrawn, all of you. My brother won't advance you any more."

"Then my man, Lawrence, will take what they can't cover," offered Speed.

"That's right! Clean 'em good, brothers," croaked the trainer.

"If you'll step over to the bunk-house, Gabby, we'll dig up some personal perquisites and family heirlooms." Stover nodded toward his men's quarters, and Gallagher grinned joyously.

"That shore listens like a band from where I set. We aim to annex the wages, hopes, and personal ambitions of y'all, along with your talkin'-machine."

"Excuse me." Willie pushed his way forward. "How's she gettin' along?"

"Fine!"

"You mule-skinners ain't broke her?"

"No; we plays her every evenin'."

The little man shifted his feet; then allowed himself to inquire, as if regarding the habits of some dear departed friend:

"Have you chose any favorite records?"

"We all has our picks. Speakin' personal, I'm stuck on that baggage coach song of Mrs. More's."

"Mo_ray!_" Willie corrected. "M-o-r-a! Heleney Mo_ray_ is the lady's name."

"Mebbe so. Our foot-runner likes that Injun war-dance best of all." Carara smiled at Cloudy, who nodded, as if pleased by the compliment. Then it was that the Flying Heart spokesman made an inquiry in hushed, hesitating tones.

"How do you like The Holy City"—he removed his hat, as did those back of him. "As sung by Madam-o-sella Melby?"

"Rotten!" Gallagher said promptly. "That's a bum, for fair."

During one breathless instant the wizened man stood as if disbelieving his ears, the enormity of the insult robbing him of speech and motion. Then he uttered a snarl, and Stover was barely in time to intercept the backward fling of his groping hand.

"No voylence, Willie! There's ladies present."

Stover's captive ground his teeth and struggled briefly, then turned and made for the open prairie without a word.

"It's his first love," said Stover, simply. The other foreman exploded into hoarse laughter, saying:

"I didn't reckon I was treadin' on the toes of no bereafed relatif's, but them church tunes ain't my style. However, we're wastin' time, gents. Where's that bunk-house? Nothin' but money talks loud enough for me to hear. Good-day, white folks!" Gallagher saluted Miss Chapin and her friends with a flourish, and moved away in company with the cowboys.

"I never," said Glass, "seen so many tough guys outside of a street-car strike."

"Gallagher has been in prison," Jean informed him. "He's a wonderful shot."

"I knew it!"

Speed spoke up brightly: "Well, let's go back to the house and wait for Covington."

"But you were getting ready to go running," said Helen.

"No more running for me! I'm in good enough shape, eh, Larry?"

"Great! Barring the one thing."

"What's that?" queried Fresno.

"A little trouble with one of his nerve-centres, that's all. But even if it got worse during the night, Covington could run the race for him."

The Californian started. At last all was plain. He had doubted from the first, now he was certain; but with understanding came also a menace to his own careful plans. If Covington ran in Speed's place, how could he effect his rival's exposure? On the way back to the house he had to think rapidly.

Mrs. Keap was pacing the porch as the others came up, and called Speed aside; then, when they were alone, broke out, with blazing eyes:

"You said you had stopped him!"

"And I thought I had. I did my best."

"But he's coming! He'll be here any minute!"

"I suppose he learned you were here." Wally laughed.

"Then you must have told him."

"No, I didn't."

"Mr. Speed"—Roberta's cheeks were pallid and her voice trembled —"you—didn't—send that telegram—at all."

"Oh, but I did."

"You wanted him to get here in time to run in your place. I see it all now. You arranged it very cleverly, but you will pay the penalty."

"You surely won't tell Helen?"

"This minute! You wretched, deceitful man!"

Before he could say more, from the front of the house came the rattle of wheels, a loud "Whoa!" then Jean's voice, crying:

"Culver! Culver!" while Mrs. Keap clutched at her bosom and moaned.

Her companion bolted into the house and down the hall, shouting the name of his room-mate. Out through the front door he dashed headlong, in time to behold Fresno and the two girls assisting the new arrival toward the veranda. They were exclaiming in pity, and had their arms about the athlete, for Culver Covington, Intercollegiate One-Hundred-Yard Champion, was hobbling forward upon a pair of crutches.

The yell died in Speed's throat, he felt himself grow deadly faint.

"Crippled!" he gasped, and leaned against the door for support.

CHAPTER XV

In a daze, Speed saw his friend mount the porch painfully; in a daze, he shook his hand. Subconsciously he beheld Lawrence Glass come panting into view, throw up his hands at sight of Covington, and cry out in a strange tongue. When he regained his faculties he broke into the conversation harshly.

"What have you done to yourself?"

"I broke a toe," explained the athlete.

"You broke a toe?"

"He broke a toe!" wailed Glass, faintly.

"If it's nothing but a toe, it won't hurt your running." Speed seized eagerly upon the faintest hope.

"No. I'll be all right in a few weeks." Covington spoke carelessly, his eyes bent upon Jean Chapin. "You've g-got to run to-morrow."

"What!" Covington dragged his glance away from the cheeks of his sweetheart.

"I—I'm sick. You'll have to."

"Don't be an idiot, Wally. I can't walk!"

Helen explained, with the pride of one displaying her own handiwork: "Mr. Speed defends the Flying Heart to-morrow. You are just in time to see him."

"When did you learn to box, Wally?" Covington was genuinely amazed.

"I'm not going to box. It's a footrace. I'm training—been training ever since I arrived."

In his first bewilderment the latecomer might have unwittingly betrayed his friend had not Jean suddenly inquired:

"Where is Roberta?"

"Roberta!" Covington tripped over one of his crutches. "Roberta who?"

"Why, Roberta Keap, of course! She's chaperoning us while mother is away."

The hero of countless field-days turned pale, and seemed upon the point of hobbling back to "Nigger Mike's" buck-board.

"You and she are old friends, I believe?" Helen interposed.

"Yes! Oh yes!" Culver flashed his chum a look of dumb entreaty, but Speed was staring round-eyed into space, striving to read the future.

Helen started to fetch her just as the pallid chaperon was entering the door.

She shook hands with Covington. She observed that he was too deeply affected at sight of her to speak, and it awakened fresh misgivings in her mind.

"H-how d'y do! I didn't know you were—here!" he stammered.

"I thought it would surprise you!" Roberta smiled wanly, amazed at her own self-control, then froze in her tracks as Jean announced:

"Jack will be home to-night, Culver. He'll be delighted to see you!"

J. Wallingford Speed offered a diversion by bursting into a hollow laugh. Now that the world was in league to work his own downfall, it was time someone else had a touch of suffering. To this end he inquired how the toe had come to be broken.

"I broke it in Omaha—automobile accident." Culver was fighting to master himself.

"Omaha! Did you stop in Omaha?" inquired Jean.

"A city of beautiful women," Speed reflected, audibly. "Somebody step on your foot at a dance?"

"No, of course not! I don't know anybody in Omaha! I went motoring—"

"Joy-ride?"

"Not at all."

"Who was with you?" Miss Chapin's voice was ominously sweet.

"N—nobody I knew."

"Does that mean that you were alone?"

"Yes. I stopped off between trains to view the city, and took a 'Seeing Omaha' ride. The yap wagon upset, and—I broke my toe."

"You left Chicago ten days ago," said Speed accusingly.

"Of course, but—when I broke my toe I had to stay. It's a beautiful city—lots of fine buildings." "How did you like the jail?"

"What in the world are you boys talking about?" queried Miss Blake.

"Mr. Speed seems amused at Culver's accident." Roberta gave him a stinging look. "Now we'd better let Culver go to his room and freshen up a bit. I want to talk to you, Helen," and Speed drooped at the meaning behind her words. But it was time for a general conference; events were shaping themselves too rapidly for him to cope with. Once the three were alone he lost no time in making his predicament known, the while his friend listened in amazement.

"But is it really so serious?" the latter asked, finally.

"It's life or death. There's a homocidal maniac named Willie guarding me daytimes, and a pair of renegades who keep watch at my window all night. The cowboys bathe me in ice-water to toughen me, and feed me raw meat to make me wild. In every corner there lurks an assassin with orders to shoot me if I break training, every where I go some low-browed criminal feels my biceps, pinches my legs, and asks how my wind is. I tell you, I'm going mad."

"And the worst part of it is," spoke Glass, sympathetically, "they'll bump me off first. It's a pipe."

"But, Wally, you can't run."

"Don't I know it?"

"Don't I?" seconded the trainer.

"Then why attempt the impossible? Call the race off."

"It's too late. Don't you understand? The bets are made, and its 'pay or play.' The cowboys have mortgaged their souls on me."

"He was makin' a play for that little doll—"

"Don't you call Miss Blake a doll, Larry! I won't stand for it!"

"Well, 'skirt,' then."

"Why don't you cut it? There's a train East at midnight."

"And leave Helen—like that? Her faith in me has weakened already; she'd hate me if I did that. No! I've got to face it out!"

"They'll be singin' hymns for both of us," predicted the fat man.

"I don't care. They can boil me in oil—I won't let her think I'm a coward."

"Larry doesn't have to stay."

"Of course not. He can escape."

"Not a chance," said the trainer. "They watch me closer 'n they do him."

Covington considered for a moment. "It certainly looks bad, but perhaps the other fellow can't run either. Who is he?"

"A cook named Skinner."

"Happy name! Well, two-thirds of a sprint is in the start. How does Wally get in motion, Lawrence?"

"Like a sacred ox." Glass could not conceal his contempt.

"I'll give him some pointers; it will all help." But Speed was nervous and awkward—so awkward, in fact, that the coach finally gave it up as a bad job, saying:

"It's no use, Wally, you've got fool feet."

"I have, eh? Well, I didn't break them getting out of jail."

"The less said about that jail the better. I'm in trouble myself."

Speed might have explained that his chum's dilemma was by no means so serious as he imagined, had not watchman Willie thrust his head through the open window at that moment with the remark:

"Time to get busy!"

"We'll be right with you!" Glass seized his protege by the arm and bore him away, muttering: "Stick it out, brother, we're nearin' the end!"

Again Speed donned his running-suit and took to the road for his farewell practise. Again Willie followed at a distance on horseback, watching the hills warily. But all hope had fled from the Yale man now, and he returned to his training-quarters disheartened, resigned.

He was not resigned, however, to the visit he received later from Miss Helen Blake. That young lady rushed in upon him like a miniature cyclone, sweeping him off his feet by the fury of her denunciation, allowing him no opportunity to speak, until, with a half-sob, she demanded:

"Why—why did you deceive me?"

"I love you!" Wally said, as if no further explanation were necessary.

"That explains nothing. You made sport of me! You couldn't love me and do that!"

"Helen!"

"I thought you were so fine, so strong, but you lied—yes, that is what you did! You fibbed to me the first day I met you, and you've been fibbing ever since. I could never, never care for a man who would do that."

"Who has told you these things?"

"Roberta, for one. She opened my eyes to your—baseness."

"Well, Roberta has a grudge against my sex. She's engaged to all the men she hasn't already married. Marriage is a habit with her. It has made her suspicious—"

"But you did deceive me, didn't you?"

"Will you marry me?" asked J. Wallingford Speed.

"The idea!" Miss Blake gasped. "Will you?"

"Please don't speak that way. When a man cares for a woman, he doesn't deceive her—he tells her everything. You told me you were a great runner, and I believed you. I'll never believe you again. Of course, I shall behave to you in a perfectly friendly manner, but underneath the surface I shall be consumed with indignation." Miss Blake commenced to be consumed. "See! You don't acknowledge your perfidy even now."

"What's the use? If I said I couldn't run, and then beat the cook, you'd believe I deceived you again. And suppose that I can't beat him?"

"Then I shall know they have told me the truth."

"And if, on the other hand, I should win"—Miss Blake's eyes fell—"Helen, would you marry me?" Speed started toward her, but she had fled out into the twilight.

Dusk was settling over stretches of purple land, and already the room was peopled by shadows. Work was over; there were sounds of cheerful preparations for supper; from the house came faint chords of laughter; a Spanish song floated in, as Carara told his love to the tune of Mariedetta's guitar:

"'Adios! adios! adios! por siempre,
Adios! coqueta, mi amor;
Adios! adios! adios! por siempre,
Adios! coqueta, mi amor!'"

It was the hush that precedes the evening as it does the dawn; the hour of reverie, in which all music is sweet, and forgotten faces arise to haunt.

Speed stood where the girl had left him, miserable, hopeless, helpless; the words of the Spanish song seemed sung for a lost love of his. And certainly his love was lost. He had stayed on in the stubborn superstitious belief that something would surely happen to relieve him from his predicament—fortune had never failed him before—and instead, every day, every incident, had served to involve him deeper. Now she knew! It was her golden heart that had held her true thus far, but could any devotion survive the sight of humiliation such as he would suffer on the morrow? Already he heard the triumphant jeers of the Centipede henchmen, the angry clamor of the Flying Heart, the mocking laughter of his rival.

He groaned aloud. Forsooth, a broken toe! Of all the countless tens of thousands of toes in Christendom, the one he had hung his salvation upon had proven weaker than a reed. What cruel jest of Fate was this? If Fate had wished to break a toe, why had she not selected, out of all the billions at her disposal, that of some other athlete than Culver Covington—even his own.

J. Wallingford Speed started suddenly and paled. He had remembered that no one could force a crippled man to run.

"By Jove," he exclaimed, "I'll do it!"

He crossed quickly to the bunk-house door and looked in. The room was empty. The supper-bell pealed out, and he heard the cow-men answer it. Now was the appointed moment; he might have no other. With cat-like tread he slipped into the sleeping-quarters, returning in a moment with a revolver. He stared thankfully at the weapon—better this than dishonor.

"Why didn't I think of it before? It's perfectly simple. I'll accidentally shoot myself—in the foot."

But even as he gazed at the gun he saw that the muzzle was as large as a gopher-hole. A bullet of that size would sink a ship, he meditated in a panic, and as for his foot—what frightful execution it would work! But—it were better to lose a foot than a foot-race, under present conditions, so he began to unlace his shoe. Then realizing the value of circumstantial evidence, he paused. No! His disability must bear all the earmarks of an accident. He must guess the location of his smallest and least important toe, and trust the rest to his marksmanship. Visions of blood-poisoning beset him, and when he pressed the muzzle against the point of his shoe his hand shook with such a palsy that he feared he might miss. He steeled himself with the thought that other men had snuffed out life itself in this manner, then sat down upon the floor and cocked the weapon a second time. He wondered if the shock might, by any chance, numb him into unconsciousness. If so, he might bleed to death before assistance arrived. But he had nothing to do with that. The only question was, which foot. He regarded them both tenderly. They were nice feet, and had done him many favors. He loved every toe; they were almost like innocent children. It was a dastardly deed to take advantage of them thus, but he advanced the revolver until it pressed firmly against the outside of his left foot, then closed his eyes, and called upon his courage. There came a great roaring in his ears.

How long he sat thus waiting for the explosion he did not know, but he opened his eyes at length to find the foot still intact, and the muzzle of the weapon pointing directly at his instep. He altered his aim hurriedly, when, without warning of any sort, a man's figure appeared silhouetted against the window.

The figure dropped noiselessly to the floor inside the room, and cried, in a strange voice:

"Lock those doors! Quick!"

Finding that it was no hallucination, Speed rose, calling out:

"Who are you?"

"Sh-h-h!" The stranger darted across the room and bolted both doors, while the other felt a chill of apprehension at these sinister precautions. He grasped his revolver firmly while his heart thumped.

The fellow's appearance was anything but reassuring: he was swarthy and sun-browned, his clothes were ragged, his overalls were patched; instead of a coat, he wore a loosely flapping vest over a black sateen shirt, long since rusted out to a nondescript brown.

"I've been trying to get to you for a week," announced the mysterious visitor hoarsely.

"W-what do you want? Who are you?"

"I'm Skinner, cook for the Centipede."

"The man I race?"

"Not so loud." Skinner was training for the faintest sound from the direction of the mess-house.

"I'll kill him!" exulted the Eastern lad. But the other forestalled a murder by running on, rapidly:

"Listen, now! Humpy and I jobbed this gang last month; we're pardners, see? He's got another race framed at Pocatello, and I want to make a get-away—"

"Yes! yes! y-you needn't stay here—on my account."

"Now don't let's take any chances to-morrow, see? We're both out for the coin. What do you want to do—win or lose?" Skinner jumped back to the door and listened.

"What?"

"Don't stall!" the stranger cried, impatiently. "Will I win or will you? What's it worth?" He clipped his words short, his eyes darted furtive glances here and there.

"Can I win?" gasped Speed.

"You can if there's enough in it for me. I'm broke, see? You bet five hundred, and we'll cut it two ways."

"I-I haven't that much with me."

"Borrow it. Don't be a boob. Meet me in Albuquerque Sunday, and we'll split there."

"Is that all I have to do?"

"Certainly. What's the matter with you, anyhow?" Skinner cast a suspicious glance at his companion.

"I-I guess I'm rattled—it's all so sudden."

"Of course you'll have to run, fast enough so we don't tip off."

"How fast is that?"

"Oh, ten-four," carelessly. "That's what Humpy and I did."

"Ten and four-fifths-seconds?"

"Certainly. Don't kid me! They're liable to break in on us." Skinner stepped to the window, but Speed halted him with a trembling hand and a voice of agony.

"Mr. Skinner, I-I can't run that fast. F-fifteen is going some for me."

"What!" Skinner stared at his opponent strangely. "That's right. I'm a lemon."

"Ain't you the Yale champ? The guy that goes under 'even time'?"

Wally shook his head. "I'm his chum. I couldn't catch a cramp."

The brown face of the Centipede sprinter split into a grin, his eyes gleamed. "Then I'll win," said he. "I'm the sucker, but I'll make good. Get your money down, and I'll split with you."

"No, no! Not you! Me! I must win!" Speed clutched his caller desperately.

"All right, I'll frame anything; but I can't run any slower than I did with Joe and make a live of it. They'd shoot us both."

"But there's a girl in this-a girl I love. It means more than mere life."

Skinner was plainly becoming nervous at the length of the interview.

"Couldn't you fall down?" inquired the younger man, timidly.

The cook laughed derisively. "I could fall down twice and beat you in fifteen." After an instant's thought:

"Say, there's one chance, if we don't run straight away. There's a corral out where we race; you insist on running around it, see? There's nothing in the articles about straight-aways. That'll kid 'em on the time. If I get too far ahead, I'll fall down."

"B-but will you stay down? Till I catch up?"

"Sure! Leave it to me."

"You won't forget, or anything like that?"

"Certainly not. But no rough work in front of the cowboys, understand? Sh-h!"

Skinner vaulted lightly through the window, landing in the dirt outside without a sound. "Somebody coming," he whispered. "Understand Merchants' Hotel, Albuquerque, noon, Sunday." And the next instant he had vanished into the dusk, leaving behind him a youth half hysterical with hope.

Out of the blackest gloom had come J. Wallingford Speed's deliverance, and he did not pause to consider the ethics involved. If he had he would have told himself that by Skinner's own confession the Centipede had won through fraud at the first race; if they were paid back in their own coin now it would be no more than tardy justice. With light heart he hastened to replace the borrowed revolver in the bunk-room just as voices coming nearer betokened the arrival of his friends from the house. As he stepped out into the night he came upon Jack Chapin.

"Hello, Wally!"

"Hello, Jack!" They shook hands, while the owner of the Flying Heart continued.

"I've just got in, and they've been telling me about this foot-race. What in the deuce is the matter with you, anyhow? Why didn't you let me know?"

The girls drew closer, and Speed saw that Miss Blake was pale.

"I wouldn't have allowed it for a minute. Now, of course, I'm going to call it off."

"Oh, Jack, dear, you simply can't!" exclaimed his sister. "You've no idea the state the boys are in."

"They'll never let you, Chapin," supplemented Fresno.

The master laughed shortly. "They won't, eh? Who is boss here, I'd like to know?"

"They've bet a lot of money. And you know how they feel about that phonograph."

"It's the most idiotic thing I ever heard of. Whatever possessed you, Wally? If the men make a row, I'll have to smuggle you and Glass over to the railroad to-night."

"I'm for that," came the voice of Larry.

"I suppose it's all my fault," Miss Blake began wretchedly, whereat the object of their general solicitude took on an aspect of valor.

"Say, what is all this fuss about? I don't want to be smuggled anywhere, thank you!"

"I may not be able to square my men," Chapin reiterated. "It may have gone too far."

"Square! Square! Why should you do any squaring? I'm not going to run-away." Miss Blake clasped her hands and breathed a sigh. "I've got to stay here and run a foot-race to-morrow."

"Don't be a fool, Wally!" Covington added his voice to the others.

Speed whirled angrily. "I don't need your advice—convict!" The champion hobbled hastily out of range. "I know what I'm doing. I'm going to run to-morrow, and I stand a good chance to win."

Mr. Fresno, if he had been a girl, would have been said to have giggled.

"All right, Dearie! I'll bet you five hundred dollars—" as there emerged from the darkness, whence they had approached unseen, Stover, and behind him the other men.

"Evenin'! What's all the excitement?" greeted the leader, softly.

The master of the ranch stepped forward.

"See here, Bill, I'm sorry, but I won't stand for this foot- race."

"Why not?" queried the foreman.

"I just won't, that's all. You'll have to call it off."

"I'm sorry, too."

"You refuse?" The owner spoke ominously.

"You bet he does!" Willie pushed himself forward. "This foot-race is ordained, and it comes off on time. I make bold to inquire if you're talkin' for our runner?"

"Gentlemen, I can only say to you that for myself I want to run!" declared Speed.

"Then you'll run."

"I refuse to allow it," Chapin declared, and instantly there was an angry murmur; but before it could take definite form, Speed spoke up with equal decisiveness.

"You can't refuse to let me run, Jack. There are reasons"—he searched Miss Blake's countenance—"why I must run—and win. And win I shall!" Turning, he stalked away into the darkness, and there followed him a shout of approbation from the ranchmen.

Jack Chapin threw up his hands.

"I've done my best."

"The man's mad!" cried Covington, but Fresno was nearer the truth. "Nothing of the sort," he remarked, and struck a match; "he's bluffing!"

As for Helen Blake, she shook her fair head and smiled into the night.

"You are all wrong," she said. "I know!"

CHAPTER XVI

The day of the race dawned bright and fair, without a cloud to mar its splendor. As the golden morning wore on, a gradual excitement became apparent among the cowboys, increasing as the hours passed, and as they prepared with joy to invade their rival's territory; nevertheless, the vigilant watch upon their champion did not relax. Theirs was an attitude of confidence tinged with caution.

It was some time after midnight that Lawrence Glass had been the cause of a wild alarm that brought the denizens of the ranch out in night apparel. Jack Chapin, awakened by a cry for help, had found him in the hands of Carara and Cloudy, who had been doing night duty in accordance with Stover's orders. What with the trainer's loud complaints, the excited words of his captors, and the confusion resulting when the bunk-house emptied itself of men half clad, it had taken the ranch-owner some time to discover that Glass had been surprised in the act of escaping. It seemed that the sentries, seeing a figure skulking past the white adobe walls of the house, had called upon it to halt. There had been a dash for liberty, then a furious struggle before the intruder's identity became clear, and but for Chapin's prompt arrival upon the scene violence would inevitably have resulted. As it was, the owner had difficulty in restraining his men, who saw in this significant effort a menace to their hopes.

"I tell you, I'm walkin' in my sleep," declared Glass for the twentieth time.

"Caramba! You try for get away," stormed the Mexican. "Pig!"

"Not a bit like it! I've been a sonnambulust ever since I'm a baby."

"Why didn't you answer when we called?" Cloudy demanded.

"How can I talk when I'm sound asleep?"

"If you couldn't hear us call, why did you run?"

"Now have a little sense, pal. A sleep-walker don't know what he's doin'."

"Since there's no harm done, you'd better all go back to bed," Chapin advised. "Mr. Glass has the liberty of the ranch, boys, night or day, asleep or awake."

"Looks to me like he was tryin' to elope some." Stover balanced upon one bare foot, and undertook to remove a sand-burr from the other. In the darkness he seemed supernaturally tall, so that Glass hastened to strengthen his story.

"I was walkin' in my sleep as nice as you please when those rummies lep' on me. Say! You know that's dangerous; you can kill a guy wakin' him up so sudden."

"There's easier ways than that," spoke Willie from the gloom.

"It's a yap trick just the same. I was in the middle of a swell dream, too."

"Come, come, Stover, get your boys back to bed! We'll have the whole ranch up with this noise."

Chapin himself led Glass around the house, while that gentleman made no offer to explain the dream which had prompted him to pack his suit-case before letting himself out of the training-quarters. Once safely back in the gymnasium, he sat up till dawn, a prey to frightful visions which the comfortable morning light did not serve to dissipate.

Wally Speed slept serenely through the whole disturbance, and was greatly amused at the story when he awoke. He was sorely tempted to make known his agreement with Skinner, and put an end to his trainer's agony of mind; but he recalled Skinner's caution, and reflected that the slightest indiscretion might precipitate a tragedy. For the first time since the beginning of the adventure he was perfectly at ease, and the phenomenon added to his trainer's dismay.

Others beside Lawrence Glass were apprehensive. Culver Covington, for instance, was plainly upset, while Roberta Keap pleaded headache and had her breakfast served in her room.

It was shortly afterward that she appeared in the gymnasium doorway, and cried, in an accusing voice:

"Well, Mr. Speed!"

"Yes, quite well."

"You traitor!"

"You modern Borgia! Didn't you go and tell Helen everything?"

"Didn't you promise to stop Culver?"

"I did. I had him thrown in jail at Omaha. What more could I do?"

"You did try? Honestly?" Mrs. Keap allowed her indignation to abate slightly. "If I had known that, I wouldn't have told Helen. I'm sorry you didn't explain. I was angry—furious. And I was frightened so!" She broke down suddenly. "What shall I do about them? I can see what they want to say, and yet I daren't let either speak a word."

"Mrs. Keap, are you sure Culver loves you?"

"Horribly! And he suspects the truth. I saw him change the moment he found me here." Roberta began to weep; two limpid tears stole down her cheeks, she groped for a chair, and Wally hastened to her assistance. As he supported her, she gave way completely and bowed her head upon his shoulder.

It was in perfect keeping with the luck of things that Miss Blake should enter at the moment. She had come with Jack and his sister to inquire regarding the fitness of her champion and to nerve him for the contest, and she stood aghast. Chapin stepped forward with a look of suspicion, inquiring:

"What's going on here?"

Miss Blake spoke brightly, tinkling ice in her voice.

"There's no necessity for an explanation, is there? It seems time for congratulations."

"Oh, see here now! Mrs. Keap's really engaged to Culver, you know."

"Culver!"

"Culver!"

Both the young ranchman and his sister stared at the chaperon with growing horror, while she undertook to explain; but the blow had fallen so swiftly that her words were incoherent, and in the midst of them her hostess turned and fled from the room.

"Now don't begin to aviate until you understand the truth," Speed continued. "While she's engaged to that broken-toed serpent, she doesn't love him, do you see?" He smiled.

"I do not see!"

"It was simply a habit Mrs. Keap had got into—I should say it was an impulsive engagement that she has repented of."

"No doubt she was repenting when we interrupted you," said Miss Blake, bitterly.

Then Chapin added, helplessly: "But Culver is engaged to my sister Jean!"

"Jean!" Mrs. Keap exposed her tragic face. "Then—he deceived me! Oh-h! What wretches men are!" The widow commenced to sob.

Outside came Miss Chapin's voice: "So here you are, Mr. Covington!" And the next moment she reappeared, dragging the crippled champion behind her. Thrusting him toward Roberta, she pouted: "There, Mrs. Keap! I give him back to you."

"Perhaps you'd better go on with your explanations," Chapin suggested, coldly, to Speed.

"How can I when you won't listen to me? Hear ye! Hear ye! Culver was engaged to marry Mrs. Keap, but she discovered what a reprobate he is—"

There was indistinguishable dissent of some sort from Mr. Covington.

"—and she learned to detest him!"

Mrs. Keap likewise dissented in accents muffled.

"Well, she would have learned to detest him in a short time, because she's in love with Jack Chapin; so she came to old Doctor Speed in her troubles, and he promised to fix it all up. Now I guess you four can do the rest of the explaining. Let this be a lesson to all of you. If you ever get in trouble, come to the match-making kid. I'll square it."

They were four happy young people, and they lost no time in escaping elsewhere. When they had gone, their benefactor said to Miss Blake:

"Wouldn't you like to make that a triple wedding? We might get club rates."

For answer Miss Blake hurried to the door and was gone.

Over at the Centipede there was a great activity and yet a certain idleness also, as if it had been a holiday. The men hung about in groups listening to the peripatetic phonograph. A dozen or more outsiders had ridden over from the post-office to witness the contest. Out by the corral, which stood close to the first break of the foot-hills, Skinner was superintending the laying out of a course, selecting a stretch of level ground worn smooth and hard by the tread of countless hoofs.

"Makes a pretty good track, eh?" he said to Gallagher. "I wonder how fast this feller is? Ever heard?"

"They seem to think he's a whirlin' ball of fire, but that don't worry you none, does it?" Gallagher bent his lead-blue eyes upon the cook, who shrugged carelessly, and Gallagher smiled; he was forced to admit that his man did not appear to be one easily frightened. Skinner's face was hard, his lips thin, his jaw was not that of a weakling. He had dressed early, then wrapped a horse-blanket about his shoulders, and now, casting this aside, sprinted down the dirt track for a few yards to test the footing, while Gallagher watched him with satisfaction—a thing of steel and wire, as tough, as agile, and as spirited as a range-raised cow-pony. He was unshaven, his running-trunks were cut from a pair of overalls, held up at the waist by a section of window-cord, and his chest was scantily covered by an undershirt from which the sleeves had been pulled. But when he returned to pick up his blanket Gallagher noted approvingly that he was not even breathing heavily. With a knowledge confined mainly to live-stock, the foremen inquired:

"How's your laigs? I like to see 'em hairy, that-a-way; it's a sign of stren'th. I bet this college boy is as pink as a maiden's palm! He don't look to me like he could run."

"They fool you sometimes," said Skinner. "By-the-way, what have you bet?"

"We laid the phonograph agin their treasures an' trappin's—"

"But how much money?"

"We got three hundred pesos down, but they sent word they was comin' loaded for b'ar, so we rustled five hundred more."

Skinner's eyes gleamed. "I wish I had a couple of hundred to bet on myself."

"Broke, eh?"

"I'm as clean as a hound's tooth."

"I'm sorry y'all tossed off your wages, but"—Gallagher started suspiciously—"say! I reckon that won't affect your runnin' none, will it?"

Skinner admitted that he could run best when he had something to run for. "You might advance me a month's wages," he reflected.

"I'll do it. Hello! Say, ain't that one of them Flyin' Heart city visitors?" From the direction of the ranch buildings Berkeley Fresno was approaching.

"Good-afternoon! You are Mr. Gallagher, I believe? I rode over with our crowd just now." Fresno looked back. "Let's step around to the other side of the corral; I want to talk to you." He led the way; then inquired, "Is this your runner?"

"That's him. His name's Skinner, and that's a promisin' title to bet on." Gallagher slipped a roll of bank-notes from his pocket. "Unhook! I'll bet you."

"No, no! I think myself Mr. Skinner will win. That's why I'm here."

"Strip your hand, son. I don't savvy."

And Fresno explained.

"You see, I'm a guest over there; but there's no sentiment with me in money matters." He produced a wallet, and took from it five one-hundred-dollar bills. "Bet this for me, and don't let on where it came from. I'll see you after the race. Mind you, not a word!"

"I'm dumb as the Egyptian Spinks."

"This race means a lot to me, Mr. Skinner." The guest of the Flying Heart Ranch turned to its enemy. "There's a girl in it. Understand?" The cook showed the gleam of his teeth. "If you win, I'll send you some wedding-cake and—a box of cigars."

"Thanks," said the other; "but I've got a bum tooth, and I don't smoke."

As Fresno left, there approached, in a surging group, the opposing side.

"Good-evenin', Gabby!" Stover called, loudly, as he came within speaking distance. "Here we come en massay, and with ladies, to further embarrass and degrade you in the hour of your defeat!"

"We ain't defeated yit! How do, Mr. Chapin."

"Did you get our message?"

"Yes. But we ain't seen the color of y'all's money."

"Mr. Speed borrowed five hundred dollars from me, and said he might want more," Chapin volunteered.

"Is that all?"

"All?" jeered Still Bill. "Why, this mangy layout ain't never saw that much money," upon which Gallagher carelessly displayed a corpulent roll of bills, remarking:

"Count a thousand, Bill. It all goes on Skinner."

"I ain't heard of no train-robbery," muttered the lanky foreman of the Flying Heart, "nor I don't aim to handle no' tainted money." And Stover and Gallagher faced each other hard before turning.

Jean saw it, and whispered to Chapin: "Oh, Jack dear, I'm terribly frightened!" But Helen Blake, who overheard, left her companions and went straight to Gallagher.

"I should like," she said, "to wager a few dollars on Mr. Speed and the honor of the Flying Heart."

Both Skinner and his foreman stared at her nonplussed.

"You don't look like a bettin' lady," the latter managed to remark, jocularly.

"I'm not, I never made a wager before in all my life; but you see, Mr. Gallagher, I believe in our man." Gallagher lowered his eyes. "How much do you aim to risk, miss?"

"I don't know what the rules are, but I think our side ought to bet as much as your side. That is the way it is done, isn't it?"

"You mean that you aim to cover what Mr. Speed don't?" The girl nodded.

Gallagher spoke admiringly. "You're right game, miss, but I reckon we don't want your money."

"Why not?"

"I suppose there ain't no partic'lar reason."

"If Mr. Speed can beat Mr. Covington, who is the best runner at Yale, I'm sure he can defeat Mr. Skinner, who never went to college at all. They have all turned against him, and he-he is so brave!" Miss Blake's indignation was tearful, and Gallagher spoke hurriedly:

"He may be brave all right, miss, but he can't win unless Skinner dies. You save your money to buy chocolates an' bon-mots, miss. Why, listen" (the stock man softened his voice in a fatherly manner): "this Fresno party is wise; five hundred of this coin is his."

Helen uttered a cry. "Do you mean he is betting against Mr. Speed?"

"Nothin' else."

"Despicable!" breathed the girl. "Wait a moment, please!" Helen hurried back to Chapin, while Gallagher muttered something like "I ain't takin' no orphan's money."

"Jack!" (the girl was trembling with excitement), "you told me on the way over that you had five hundred dollars with you. Let me have it, please. I'll give you my check when we get home."

"My dear girl, you aren't going to — bet it?"

"Yes, I am."

"Don't do that!"

For answer she snatched the pocket-book from his hand.

"Mr. Gallagher!" she called.

Skinner watched from afar. "Some class to that gal!" was what he said, which proved that he was a person not wholly without sentiment.

CHAPTER XVII

Speed leaped down from the buck-board in which Carara had driven him and Glass over to the Centipede corral.

"I told you to jump out when we crossed that bridge," was Larry's reproach to him. "You could have broke your arm. Now — it's too late."

But Speed joined his friends with the most cheerful of greetings.

They responded nervously, shocked at his flippant assurance.

"This, Mr. Speed, is the scene of your defeat!" Gallagher made the introduction.

"And this is Mr. Skinner, no doubt?" Wally shook hands with the Centipede runner, who stared at him, refused to recognize his knowing wink, and turned away. "You think pretty well of yourself, don't you?" suggested Gallagher unpleasantly, and Speed laughed. There was no reason why he should not laugh. Either way his hour had come.

"I s'pose that satchel is full of money?" Gallagher pointed to the suitcase.

"On the contrary, it is full of clothes. It is I who contain the money." He thrust a cold palm into his pocket as Covington dragged him aside to advise him not to be an utter idiot, to throw his money away if he must, but to throw it to charity or to his friends.

"Yes," Glass seconded, lugubriously, "and hold out enough to buy me a Gates Ajar in immortelles." But he said also, as if to himself, "He may be wrong in the burr, but he's a game little guy."

As the Centipede foreman counted the money, Helen came forward, announcing:

"You'll have to win now, won't you, Mr. Speed? I've wagered five hundred dollars on you. I bet against Mr. Fresno." "Fresno! So he's out from cover at last, eh?"

"I haven't been under cover," spoke up the Californian. "I've been wise all along."

Chapin wheeled. "Does it seem to you quite the thing to bet against our man, Fresno?" he inquired, his glance full in the other's eyes.

"Why not? There's no sentiment in financial affairs."

Speed shrugged. "Our tenor friend will sing his way back to California." He turned with his thanks to Helen.

"The talkin'—machine!" interrupted Still Bill, suddenly. A group of men was approaching, who bore the phonogragh upon a dry-goods box, and deposited it in state beside the race-course. "Say, Gabby, s'pose you give us a tune, just to show she's in good order."

"Suspicious, eh?"

"You bet! There's a monologue I'd admire to hear. It's called-"

"We'll have The Holy City," said Willie, positively. "It's more appropriate."

So, with clumsy fingers, Gallagher fitted a record, then wound up the machine under the jealous eyes of the Flying Heart cowboys.

Drawn by the sound, Skinner, wrapped to the chin in his blanket, idled toward the crowd, affording Glass a sight of his face for the first time. The latter started as if stung, and crying under his breath, "Salted car-horse!" drew his employer aside.

"Say," he said, pointing a finger, "who's that?"

"Skinner, the man I run."

Glass groaned. "His name ain't Skinner; that's 'Whiz' Long. Six years ago I saw him win the Sheffield Handicap from scratch in nine-three." Then, as Speed did not seem to be particularly pressed, "Don't you understand, Wally? He's a pro; this is his game!"

To which the younger man replied, serenely and happily, "It's fixed."

"What's fixed?"

"The race. It's all arranged—framed."

"Who framed it? How? When?"

"Sh-h! I did. Yesterday; by stealth; I fixed it."

"You win from 'Whiz' Long, and you can't run under fifteen?"

Wally nodded. "I told him that—it's all right."

"You told him?" Glass staggered. "It's all right? Say! Don't you know he's the fastest, crookedest, cheatingest, double-crossingest—why, he just came to feel you out!"

And Speed turned dizzy.

"And you fell for that old stuff!" Larry's voice was trembling with anger and disgust. "Why, that's part of his 'work.' He's double-crossed every runnin' mate he ever had. He'd cheat his mother. Wait!"

Skinner had left the crowd, and was seated now in the shade of the corral fence. He glanced upward from beneath his black brows as Larry reached and greeted him. "Hello, Whiz! I just 'made' you—" Then he shook his head.

"I haven't got you. My name is Skinner."

"Nix on that monaker," Glass smiled, indulgently. "I had a man in that Sheffield Handicap six years ago."

"You're in bad," asserted the cook steadily, "but assuming that my name is Long—"

"I didn't say your name was 'Long.' I called you 'Whiz.'" Glass chuckled at the point as he scored it. "Now come in; be good."

Skinner darted a look toward Gallagher and the Centipede men gathered about the shrilling phonograph, stooped and tied his shoes, and breathed softly:

"Spiel!"

"This little feller I'm trainin'—does he win?"

Without an upward glance, Skinner inquired:

"Did the man you trained for the Sheffield Handicap win?"

"Never mind that. Does this frame-up go through?" It happened that Speed, drawn irresistibly, had come forward to hang upon every word, and now chose this moment to interrupt.

"It's all right, Mr. Skinner—" But Skinner leaped to his feet.

"Don't try anything like that!" he cried, in a terrible voice that brought Gabby Gallagher striding toward them.

"What's goin' on here? Are they try in' to fix you, Skinner?"

"Not a bit like it," Glass protested stoutly. "I only asked him which side he'd rather run on, and now he calls for police protection."

"Don't try it again, that's all!" the cook warned, sullenly.

"I reckon I'll take a hand in this!" Gallagher was in a fine rage, and would have fallen upon the offender had not Stover stepped in his path.

"I reckon you won't!" he said easily.

The two glared at each other, and were standing thus when Speed and his trainer moved gently off. They made their way to the house in comparative silence. "I—I made a mistake," said Wally.

"You've been jobbed like you was a baby," said Glass. "There ain't but one thing to do now. Go into the house and change your clothes, and when you get ready to run, get ready to run for your life—and mine." Over on the race-course Gallagher was inquiring:

"Who's goin' to send these y'ere athaletes away?"

"I am!" announced Willie without hesitation "Bein' perhaps the handiest man present with a weepon, I'm goin' to start this journey." He looked his foes squarely in the eyes. "Has anybody got objections to me?" The silence was nattering, and more loudly now, so that Skinner might hear, he added: "If your man tries to beat the gun, I'll have him wingin' his way to lands celestial before he makes his second jump."

Gallagher acknowledged the fairness of this proposition. "This race is goin' to be squar'," said he. "We're ready when y'all are."

J. Wallingford Speed stepped out of his clothes and into his silken running-suit. He was numb and cold. His hands performed their duties to be sure, but his brain was idle. All he knew was that he had been betrayed and all was lost. He heard Glass panting instructions into his ear, but they made no impression upon him. In a dull trance he followed his trainer back to the track, his eyes staring, his bones like water. Not until he heard the welcoming shout of the Flying Heart henchmen did he realize that the worst was yet to come. He heard Larry still coaching earnestly: "If you can't bite him, trip him up," and some one said:

"Are we ready?"

Glass held out his hand. "Good-bye, Mr. Speed."

Chapin came forward and spoke with artificial heartiness, "Good-luck, Wally; beat him at the start," and Covington followed.

"Remember," he cautioned, sadly, "what I told you about the start—it's your only chance."

"Why don't you fellows think about the finish of this race?" faltered the runner.

Then, in a voice broken with excitement, Helen Blake spoke, holding out her hand for a good-bye clasp. "Dear Mr. Speed," she said, "will you try to remember this?—remember to run before he does, and don't let him catch up to you. If you do that, I just know you'll win."

This magnificent display of confidence nerved the athlete, and he smiled at her. He wished to speak, but dared not trust himself.

Gallagher was calling; so he went to the starting-point, whence he surveyed the course. There it lay, no more than a lane leading down between ranks of brown-faced men whose eyes were turned upon him. On the top rail of the corral perched Willie, revolver in hand. The babble of voices ceased, the strident laughter stilled, Speed heard the nervous Tustle of feminine skirts. Skinner was standing like a statue, his toe to the mark, his eyes averted.

"You'll start here and run a hundred yards out yonder to the tape," Gallagher announced.

"I refuse!" said Speed firmly.

For one breathless instant there was a hush of amazement, then a cry of rage. Still Bill Stover hurled the nearest man out of his path, and stode forward, his lean face ablaze. He wheeled and flung up his hand as if to check some hidden movement of Willie's.

"No voylence yet, Will! What d'you mean, Mr. Speed?"

Speed uttered what he knew was his final joke on earth. "I mean that I refuse to run straightaway. I'm an all-around athlete, and I must run all around something."

Amid shouts of confusion, those who had taken positions along the course came crowding back to the starting-point. Willie wrapped his legs about the top rail of the fence and drew a second revolver, while the two foremen bellowed indistinguishable threats at each other. Chapin lost no time in withdrawing his guests out of the turmoil, but Helen kept her place, her face chalky but her eyes very bright.

"What are you tryin' to hand us?" roared Gallagher.

Still Bill was quick to take a cue. "Don't get hectic!" said he. "There's nothin' in the articles about runnin' straight. Let 'em run around the corral." But at this suggestion every voice seemed to break out simultaneously.

"Humpy Joe ran straightaway," declared Gallagher.

"Yes, an' he kept at it," piped Willie. "I favor the idea of them runners comin' back where they start from."

"Listen, all of you," Speed announced. "I am going to run around and around and around this corral. If Mr. Skinner chooses to accompany me, he may trail along; otherwise I shall run alone."

"Never heerd of such a thing!" Gallagher was dancing in his excitement, but Skinner calmed him by announcing, curtly:

"I'll beat him any way he wants to run."

"You couldn't beat a rug," retorted Wally, and Glass suddenly smote his palms together, crying, blankly:

"I forgot the rug!"

"We don't want no arg'ment afterwards. Does the Centipede accept its fate?" Still Bill glared at the faces ringed about him.

"We do if Skinner says so."

"Twice around the corral," agreed Skinner. "But no accidents, understand? If he falls, I keep going."

Instantly there ensued a scramble for grand-stand seats; the cowboys swarmed like insects upon the stout fence of the corral.

"Then you'll start and finish here. Once y'all pass we'll stretch a string to yonder post, and the first man to bust it wins. Who's got a string?"

"Mr. Gallagher, won't you use my sash?" Helen quickly unfastened the long blue bow of ribbon from her cotton gown, and Gallagher thanked her, adding:

"Moreover, the winner gets it!"

For the first time, then, Skinner addressed Miss Blake.

"Hadn't you better make that the loser, miss? The winner gets the coin," and the assent came in a flashing smile from sky-blue eyes.

"Then the loser gets the ribbon!" Gallagher announced loudly, and made one end fast to the corral. "Which I call han'some treatment for Mr. Speed, an' only wish we might retain it at the Centipede as a remembrance. Are the runners ready?"

Those near the starting-line gave room. Skinner stepped quickly out from his blanket, and stamped his spikes into the soil; he raised and lowered himself on his toes to try his muscles. Speed drew his bath-robe from his shoulders and thrust it toward his trainer, who shook his head.

"Give it to Covington, Bo; I won't be here when you come back."

"Get on your marks!" The starter gave his order.

Speed set his spikes into the dirt, brought his weight forward upon his hands. He whispered something to Skinner. That gentleman straightened up, whereupon Willie cried for a second time:

"On your marks!" and again Skinner crouched.

"Get set!"

The crowd filled its lungs and waited. Helen Blake buried her nails in her rosy cold palms. Chapin and his friends were swayed by their heart-beats, while even Fresno was balanced upon his toes, his plump face eager. The click of Willie's gun sounded sharp as he cocked it.

Into the ear close by his cheek Speed again whispered an agonized—

"Don't forget to fall down!"

This time the cook of the Centipede leaped backward with an angry snarl, while the crowd took breath.

"Make him quit talking to me!" cried Skinner.

Gallagher uttered an imprecation and strode forward, only to have his way once more barred by Still Bill Stover. "He can talk if he wants to."

"There is nothing," Speed pointed out with dignity, "in the articles to forbid talking. If I wished to, I could sing. Yes, or whistle, if I felt like it."

"On your marks!" came the rasping voice of Willie as Wally murmured to Skinner:

"Remember, I trust you."

Skinner ground his teeth; the tendons in his calves stood out rigidly.

"Get set!"

Once more the silence of death wrapped the beholders, and Willie raised his arm. Speed cast one lingering farewell glance to the skies, and said, devoutly: "What a beautiful, beautiful day!"

Now the starter was shaking in an ague of fury.

"Listen, you!" he chattered, shrilly. "I'm goin' to shoot twice this time—once in the air, and the next time at the nearest foot-runner. Now, get set!" and the speaker pulled trigger, whereupon Speed leaped as if the bullet had been aimed at him.

Instantly a full-lunged roar went up that rolled away to the foot-hills, and the runners sped out of the pandemonium, their legs twinkling against the dust-colored prairie. Down to the turn they raced. Speed was leading. Fright had acted upon him as an electric charge; his terror lent him wings; he was obsessed by a propelling force outside of himself. Naturally strong, lithe, and active, he likewise possessed within him the white-hot flame of youth, and now, with a nameless fear to spurn him on, he ran as any healthy, frightened young animal would run. At the second turn Skinner had not passed him, but the thud of his feet was close behind.

This unparalleled phenomenon surprised Lawrence Glass perhaps most of all. He had laid his plans to slip quietly out of the crowd under cover of the first confusion and lay his own course eastward; but when he beheld his protege actually in the lead, he remained rooted to his tracks. Was this a miracle? He turned to Covington, to find him dancing madly, his crutches waving over his head, in his eyes the stare of a maniac. His mouth was distended, and Glass reasoned that he must be shouting violently, but could not be sure. Suddenly Covington dashed to the turn whence the runners would be revealed as they covered the last half lap, for nothing was distinguishable through the fence, burdened by human forms, and Larry lumbered after him, ploughing his way through the crowd and colliding with the box upon which stood the Echo Phonograph, of New York and Paris. He hurled Mariedetta out of his path with brutal disregard, but even before he could reach his point of vantage the sprinters burst into the homestretch. Larry Glass saw it all at a glance—Speed was weakening, while Skinner was running easily. Nature had done her utmost; she could not work the impossible. As they tore past, Skinner was ahead.

The air above the corral became blackened with hats as if a flock of vultures had wheeled suddenly; the shriek of triumph that rose from the Centipede ranks warned the trainer that he had tarried too long. Heavily he set off across the prairie for New York.

The memory of that race awakened Speed from his slumbers many times in later years. When he found the brown shoulder of his rival drawing past he realized that for him the end of all things was at hand. And yet, be it said to his credit, he held doggedly to his task, and began to fight his waning strength with renewed determination. Down through the noisy crowd he pounded at the heels of his antagonist, then out upon the second lap. But now his fatigue increased rapidly, and as it increased, so did Skinner's lead. At the second turn Wally was hopelessly outdistanced, and began to sob with fury, in anticipation of the last, long, terrible stretch. Back toward the final turn they came, the college man desperately laboring, the cook striding on like a machine. Wally saw the rows of forms standing upon the fence, but of the shouting he heard nothing. Skinner was twenty yards ahead now, and flung a look back over his shoulder. As he turned into the last straightaway he looked back again and grinned triumphantly.

Then—J. Wallingford Speed gasped, and calling upon his uttermost atom of strength, quickened the strides of his leaden legs. Skinner had fallen!

A shriek of exultation came from the Flying Heart followers; it died as the unfortunate man struggled to his feet, and was off again before his opponent had overtaken him. Down the alley of human forms the two came; then as their man drew ahead for an instant or two, such a bedlam broke forth from Gallagher's crew that Lawrence Glass, well started on his overland trip, judged that the end had come.

But Skinner wavered. His ankle turned for a second time; he seemed about to fall once more. Then he righted himself, but he came on hobbling.

The last thirty yards contained the tortures of a lifetime to Wally Speed. His lungs were bursting, his head was rolling, every step required a separate and concentrated effort of will. He knew he was wobbling, and felt his knees ready to buckle beneath him, but he saw the blue, tight-stretched ribbon just ahead, and continued to lessen the gap between himself and Skinner until he felt he must reach out wildly and grasp at the other man's clothing. Helen's face stood out from the blur, and her lips cried to him. He plunged forward, his outflung arm tore the ribbon from its fastening, and he fell. But Skinner was behind him.

CHAPTER XVIII

The only thing in the world that the victorious Speed wanted was to lie down and stretch out and allow those glowing coals in his chest to cool off. But rough hands seized him, and he found himself astride of Stover's shoulders and gyrating about the Echo Phonograph in the midst of a war-dance. He kicked violently with his spiked shoes, whereat the foreman bucked like a wild horse under the spur and dropped him, and he staggered out of the crowd, where a girl flew to him.

"Oh, Wally," she cried, "I knew you could!" He sank to the ground, and she knelt beside him.

Skinner was propped against the corral fence opposite, his face distorted with suffering, and Gallagher was rubbing his ankle.

"'Taint broke, I reckon," said Gallagher, rising. "I wish to hell it was!" He stared disgustedly at his fallen champion, and added: "We don't want y'all for a cook no more, Skinner. You never was no good nohow." He turned to Helen and handed her a double handful of bank-notes, as Berkeley Fresno buried his hands in his pockets and walked away. "Here's your coin, miss. If ever you get another hunch, let me know. An' here's yours, Mr. Speed; it's a weddin'-present from the Centipede." He fetched a deep sigh. "Thank the Lord we'll git somethin' fit to eat from now on!"

Speed staggered to Skinner, who was still nursing his injury, and held out his hand, whereat the cook winked his left eye gravely.

"The best man won," said Skinner, "and say—there's a parson at Albuquerque." Then he groaned loudly, and fell to massaging his foot.

There came a fluttering by his side, and Miss Blake's voice said to him, with sweetness and with pity: "I'm so sorry you lost your position, Mr. Skinner. You're a splendid runner!"

"Never mind the job, miss, I've got something to remember it by." He pointed to a sash which lay beside him. "The loser gets the ribbon, miss," he explained gallantly.

Off to the right there came a new outcry, and far across the level prairie a strange sight was revealed to the beholders. A fat man in white flannels was doubling and dodging ahead of two horsemen, and even from a considerable distance it could plainly be seen that he was behaving with remarkable agility for one so heavy. Repeatedly his pursuers headed him off, but he rushed past them, seemingly possessed by the blind sense of direction that guides the homing pigeon or the salmon in its springtime run. He was headed toward the east.

"Why, it's Larry!" ejaculated Speed. "And Cloudy and Carara."

"Wally, your man has lost his reason!" Chapin called.

At that instant the watchers saw the Mexican thunder down upon Glass, his lariat swinging about his head. Lazily the rope uncoiled and settled over the fleeing figure, then, amid a cloud of dust, Carara's horse set itself upon its haunches and the white-clad figure came to the end of its flight. There was a violent struggle, as if the cowboy had hooked a leaping tuna, cactus plants and sage-brush were uprooted, then the pony began to back away, always keeping the lariat taut. But Glass was no easy captive, as his threshing arms and legs betrayed, and even when he was dragged back to the scene of the race, panting, grimy, dishevelled, the rope still about his waist, he seemed obsessed by that wild insanity for flight. He was drenched with perspiration, his collar was dangling, one end of a suspender trailed behind him.

At sight of Speed he uttered a cry, then plunged through the crowd like a bull, but the lariat loop slipped to his neck and tightened like a hangman's noose.

"Larry," cried his employer, sharply, "have you lost your head?"

"Ain't they g-g-got you yet?" queried the trainer in a strangling voice.

"You idiot, I won!"

"What!"

"I won—easy."

"You won!" Larry's eyes were starting from his head.

"He sure did," said Stover. "Didn't you think he could?"

Glass apprehended that look of suspicion. "Certainly!" said he. "Didn't I say so, all along? Now take that clothesline off of me; I've got to run some more."

That evening J. Wallingford Speed and Helen Blake sat together in the hammock, and much of the time her hand was in his. The breath of the hills wandered to them idly, fragrant with the odors of the open fields, the heavens were bright with dancing stars, the night itself was made for romance. From the bunk-house across the court-yard floated the voice of the beloved Echo Phonograph, now sad, now gay; now shrilling the peaceful air with Mme. Melba's Holy City, now waking the echoes with the rasping reflections of Silas on Fifth Avenue. To the spellbound audience gathered close beside it, it was divine; but deep as was their satisfaction, it could not compare with that of the tired young son of Eli. Ineffable peace and contentment were his; the whole wide world was full of melody.

"And now that I've told you what a miserable fraud I am, you won't stop loving me?" he questioned.

Helen nestled closer and shook her head. There was no need for words.

Jack Chapin came out upon the porch with the chaperon. "Well, Fresno caught his train," he told them.

"And we had such a glorious drive coming back! The night is splendid!"

"Yes, so nice and moonlight!" Wally agreed pleasantly, whereat Jack Chapin laughed.

"It's as black as pitch."

"Why, so it is!" Then as a fresh song burst forth from the very heart of the machine, he murmured affectionately: "By Jove! there goes The Baggage Coach Ahead once more! That makes ten times."

"It's a beautiful thing, isn't it?" Miss Blake sighed dreamily.

"I—I believe I'm learning to like it myself," her lover agreed. "Poor Frez!"

The bridesmaids wore white organdie and carried violets.